Airship 27 Productions

Buck Jones in the 21st Century
© 2024 Darryle Purcell

Published by Airship 27 Productions
www.airship27.com
www.airship27hangar.com

Cover and interior illustrations © 2024 Darryle Purcell

Editor: Ron Fortier
Associate Editor: Jonathan Sweet
Marketing and Promotions Manager: Michael Vance
Production Designer: Rob Davis

All rights reserved under International and Pan-American Copyright Conventions. No part of this book may be reproduced in any manner without permission in writing from the copyright holder, except by a reviewer, who may quote brief passages in a review.

ISBN: 978-1-953589-64-4

Printed in the United States of America

10 9 8 7 6 5 4 3 2 1

BY DARRYLE PURCELL

CHAPTER ONE
MATINEE LESSONS

It was less than a week before Christmas of 2022 and my reality had slammed headlong into wall of Wonderland insanity. I was slumped down behind some rocks in the mountains of western Arizona while fatigue-wearing thugs blasted away at me with their Uzis. Pebbles rained down on my head as 9mm bullets ripped into the rocks above me.

I probably shouldn't have been surprised I was under attack, since I had just witnessed a warning of death delivered by a horrifying, shroud-wearing, grizzled old crone with sharp teeth, long fingers and empty white eyes just a half-day's ride from the appropriately named Wailing Banshee Ranch.

Although we were able to return fire with our AR-15s, my friends and I were outnumbered and outgunned by the thugs who were advancing toward our positions and getting close to being within hand-grenade range. There were five of us doing our best to stay alive, including a ranch owner, two scientists, myself and a motion picture cowboy star most people believed had died 80 years earlier. Another friend, who had a questionable sense of humor and a mysterious background, had vanished as soon as the villains arrived, claiming he was going to get help. When first blood splattered the forest ground, I realized our time was up. That's when the winged dragons started swooping out of the night sky.

As death and destruction whirled around me like a SYFY channel tornado movie, with or without sharks, my mind tried to comprehend how life had changed in a matter of a few days. The world had been a lot simpler for me when my idea of a good adventure was taking my nephew on a trip to an old-time Saturday matinee double feature.

●●●

The three mounted cowboys looked out of the flickering black and white, projected film directly at the audience, waved and said, "So long, Rough Riders," and they turned and rode in separate directions into the distance. The curtains closed in front of the screen, the lights went on and the audience cheered.

I felt uplifted, refreshed by the simple morality lesson taught by western film greats Col. Tim McCoy, Raymond Hatton and Buck Jones. And, from the looks on their faces as they left the auditorium, the rest of the audience was as thrilled as I was at that Saturday matinee presentation. They were smiling, laughing and talking about the wonderful action scenes. Some even skipped through the door on the way back to their realities. Of course, those were the ones who weren't using canes or walkers.

At 38, I was probably the second youngest member of the audience that day. I'm Dave Custer, freelance columnist, failed novelist and fulltime movie buff. Almost every Saturday, I drove to the Old Timer Theatre on Fourth Street in Long Beach to join a packed house of senior citizens for the cowboy double-feature matinee. And, appreciated by all of us, there were always two or three Scrappy, Bosko or Betty Boop cartoons between the oaters.

I was usually able to talk my 10-year-old nephew Sammy into trailin' along with me to the Theatre, even though he always had a look on his face like someone being led to the guillotine. My sister Linda (his mom), hoping to get him away from the Internet for a couple of hours, had probably told him he would be doing a good deed by accompanying his daffy uncle to see the old movies. When we were kids growing up on a ranch in northern California, she liked westerns as much as I did. Her favorites were the black and white television reruns of Annie Oakley, starring Gail Davis. But when we grew up, she actually became an adult, got married, had a son and then tragedy struck her reality like a fist out of Hell. Her husband was killed in a training accident at Fort Hood. There was no turning back for Linda. She had responsibilities—Sammy, her home, bills. She lost the enjoyments of her youthful interests and replaced them with the stress of being a working single mom.

Daffy old uncle or not, I knew she needed some down time just for herself. And I was happy to have Sammy go along on my mini-excursions into the silver screen past. I loved the old black and white adventures, as they gave me a chance to try and teach my nephew about B-western film artistry that, unfortunately, is no longer a part of Hollywood culture.

His entertainment world was in full-color, wide-screen and three dimensions. When I would try to explain how dangerous the extreme riding stunts were that Hoot Gibson, Ken Maynard, Tim McCoy, Bob Steele, Tom Tyler and Buck Jones performed, Sammy would simply parrot back a description of the CGI effects from some green-screen space-opera or superhero blockbuster. "Commander Tribellum of the Concordian System is battling a Venusian gigantasaur on an ice mountain as they both tumble off a cliff, falling 3,000 feet toward the spider valley below, which is being torn apart by a meteor shower…." Well, you get the picture.

I try to explain the western-film camera operators' abilities, without the use of computers, to form black and white images of lights and shadows into dynamic visual stories. And the stories themselves were an art form. They were simple: Good is confronted by evil. The characters must learn who the villains are and they must fight them for the right reasons. Good always triumphs over evil. These moral tutorials, which are important to all of us, were played out on the silver screen in close to an hour with each flick.

The challenges film cowboy heroes faced in those old oaters were allegories of the day-to-day problems of average Americans of both the 20th and the 21st Centuries. In modern life, however, the outcomes are different—and I blame that on the demise of the B-western and its wonderful moral lessons.

Anyway, I always took Sammy to lunch at his favorite chicken-sandwich joint after the movies so we could talk about the films and anything else he was interested in. I hoped that, some day, he would understand why real cowboys racing after villains on highly trained wonder horses were more entertaining than superhero actors wearing colorful underwear while hanging from wires in front of computer-animated backgrounds.

"I liked the cartoons," Sammy said, while brushing his bright red hair out of his eyes. "But I'll bet I probably won't understand all the things the audience found funny about Betty Boop for a couple more years."

"You're a wise young man," I said, as I dipped one of my chicken fingers in some ketchup. "But what'd you think about the Rough Riders flick?"

"It was a lot of fun. Those guys are little older than some of the cowboys you bring me to see. So there was a little more talking. But I enjoyed it."

"Good. And you are right. Tim McCoy and Buck Jones had been motion picture cowboy stars for many years by the time they united in the Rough Riders series. Both had been real cowboys for quite some time before getting started in silent films. Raymond Hatton also began his career in silent flicks in every kind of film one could imagine. All three were true professionals who gave the Rough Riders B-westerns A-film quality."

We had a very enjoyable lunch discussing such important issues as, if Buck Jones sold his horse, Silver, to the Lone Ranger, why bad guys never ride white horses, if Raymond Hatton ever carried a ventriloquist dummy like Max Terhune of "The Three Mesquiteers," whether 5th grade math was really necessary and, a most intriguing question, does Wonder Woman ever get cold in the winter while running around in her costume? I found the answer to the last one less interesting than the fact that Sammy came up with the question.

It was a beautiful, sunlit afternoon as Sammy and I walked to my new Ford Fiesta for the ride back to his mom's house. Having enjoyed the matinee films and the lively lunch discussion, I was in a great mood. And, not having read the daily newspaper, I felt that all was right with the world. Unfortunately, we passed a *Los Angeles Times* news rack on our way to the car and I read the bold-faced headline at the top of the front page—"Terrorists Strike Again." All feelings of optimism instantly washed away.

I stopped to purchase a paper and read about the latest mass murder of innocent Americans by a pair of radical Muslim immigrants. A state Assemblyman, without using the words "Muslim," "terrorist," or "immigrant," demanded an immediate ban on gun sales, claiming the violence would end when "all guns are confiscated." One sidebar quoted a couple of traumatized survivors about the shooting assault that took place during a Christmas party while another explained that the Congressional leaders were arguing over whether the incident was something more than an example of "workplace violence." The modern world was anything but civilized, and many of today's elected officials were shaking in their panties, as they were so frightened of labeling a villain.

If the Rough Riders were to somehow step off the silver screen and become part of the world in December of 2022, they would be completely baffled, I thought. The film series had started not long before the December 7, 1941, bombing of Pearl Harbor. And it ended shortly after it began when McCoy, a veteran of the Great War, rejoined the military and, late in 1942, Jones was killed in the infamous Cocoanut Grove fire. They had seen America's reaction to the Japanese assault and the drastic measures that the then-united Americans engaged in to, eventually, defeat the enemy.

"What's wrong, Uncle Dave?"

Sammy had seen the change in my demeanor as I scanned the front page.

"Everything," I said, "but nothing for you to worry about. Some no-good villains hurt some innocent people in another part of the state."

"Did the good guys catch them?"

"Yes, they did. Police officers tracked them down, caught them and, in a shoot out, finished them off."

"Good! That should teach villains not to hurt people."

"Well, those two won't hurt anyone anymore. Let's just hope political morons don't hit the officers with trumped up charges of not being compassionate enough to maniacal terrorists," I said. I took a breath and, not wanting to get too deep into the subject with Sammy, added, "We'd better get going so you can tell your mom all about the westerns and cartoons you saw today."

●●●

After I dropped Sammy off I drove to Sundance Laboratories in Torrance. I had written a few columns in a series about research facilities and Sundance was next on my list.

My publisher, James Carpenter, of the *L.A. Weekly Banner*, told me he believed readers would pay good money to learn about scientific research and development going on in the county. And who was I to argue, since he signed my checks. I considered Carpenter to be a typical newspaper publisher. He always wore a suit, had a neatly trimmed beard and was rumored to have his nails professionally manicured. He showed excitement about every article that might lead to new ad sales and contempt toward any writer who turned in a news story that dealt with assault, murder, theft, arson, property destruction, protests or anything your average real estate broker wouldn't want next to his or her paid ad. And he never "rocked the boat" by allowing anything "politically incorrect" in the publication either.

I knew very little about his home life except for the fact that he invested in what he called businesses with "unrecognized potential." Sometimes he would talk about other alien concepts such as "discretionary income." As a freelance writer, all of my investment planning was a juggling process to make sure to be able to pay my bills.

One of my first business features for the paper actually won a statewide award. It was an in-depth article on a company that had developed an oil-eating bacteria to help with industrial-spill cleanups. Of course, although I attended the state luncheon when the plaques were presented, the publisher was there to accept the award, which he then hung on *his* wall. As I said, he signed my checks. And although the number of paid *Banner* subscribers couldn't fill the average cruise ship, Carpenter's ego was the size of the *L.A. Times* readership. That was illustrated by his demeaning behavior toward his employees, and the fact the bearded buffoon with the God-complex liked everyone to call him J.C. I'm just sayin'...

Surprisingly, Sundance Laboratories owner Professor Zachariah Delaney had consented to my request for a tour and interview. As I pulled into the building's parking area, I was underwhelmed. The research facility was your typical concrete box structure within an industrial park. The outside walls were painted that faded pink color that seemed to be so popular during the late 1970s. The parking lot was cracked and a variety of enthusiastic southern California weeds had struggled through the pavement to reach the smog-filtered sunlight.

Once I got inside, things become a little more interesting. The lobby was a small room with plush chairs and framed posters from old movie serials. I stopped in front of a beautifully illustrated image from the Tom Mix serial, "Miracle Rider," with Tom riding in the Firebird, a sci-fi flying machine the film's villain, Charles Middleton, used to scare a friendly Indian tribe. The

1935, 15-chapter Mascot serial was truly a classic.

"May I help you sir?" a pretty brunette receptionist asked from behind protective glass. There was something very familiar about her, I thought. But then again, perhaps it was just that I found something familiar about every pretty brunette, blonde or redhead who smiled at me. Usually, that's as far as I got. A smile.

"Hi. I'm Dave Custer, here to see Professor Delaney."

She told me to have a seat and she would notify the professor. Instead, I walked along the walls admiring the historic film posters. There was a full-size, colorful theatrical-release poster of "The Phantom Empire," with Gene Autry and Frankie Darro right next to one of Tim McCoy riding fast on a muscular white horse for "Two Fisted Law." Each framed work of art filled my mind with wonderful memories. As I coveted, I mean perused, the Commando Cody poster of "Radar Men From the Moon," a voice came from behind me.

"I believe Republic Pictures had the most fun with their futuristic ideas," the tall, balding man with a short, graying-red beard said. "I'm Prof. Delaney, Mr. Custer. I've read your work and I trust you not to do an *Enquirer/New York Times*-style assault piece on us."

"I appreciate that," I said. "And I agree about Republic. But Mascot, Monogram, Columbia and Universal had some real winners as well."

He led the way into a long, orange, arch-ceilinged hallway, which led to a conference room that would have seemed natural on the Starship Enterprise. It contained a large, oval, glass table surrounded by high-backed leather chairs.

"Have a seat, Mr. Custer," the professor said. "We'll start with some concepts."

"Call me Dave," I said.

"And you can call me Zack. The receptionist is Beth. Our research center is made up of just a few key individuals. We're like a family here and first names are all we use beyond the lobby."

"That's nice, but, Zack, I've been wondering. You haven't given any interviews to any publications that I could find. In fact, there is very little written about Sundance Laboratories other than you are a research facility. What exactly do you research and why did you agree to talk to me?"

Delaney looked toward a mirrored wall, waved and asked, "Would you like some coffee, lemonade or a soda?"

"No, I'm fine," I said.

A door opened and Beth brought in a tray with ice, two glasses and a pitcher of lemonade.

"Well, I'm going to have a glass of this," he said. "It's made out of real lemons from my backyard. Help yourself if you change your mind."

As he poured his drink I could almost hear the wheels turning in his head.

"We have several levels of activities here. Our grants allow us to delve into a variety of concepts as a scientific think tank. But we are also able to research and develop mechanical avenues regarding a few of those concepts. I'll show you some of that in a bit.

"As for you being here, you may have called us but we chose you."

"But how would you know…?"

"Your publisher has been hounding us for an interview," he said. "Once I knew you were going to be the writer, I acquiesced."

"Can you be a little more clear?" I asked.

"Certainly. As I said, I have read your work—all of it. We checked you out all the way back into your military service and schooling. You have very good communication skills and you understand certain scientific concepts and political realities."

"You did all that just so you could trust me enough to give you a little press?"

"Not exactly. We're not going to do a PR interview today. What we are going to do is to show you around, have a discussion, get to know each other a little bit and, perhaps, offer you a very good fulltime job."

That slapped me upside the head like a handful of wet 20-dollar bills. I was barely making ends meet with my freelance work for the *Banner* and a fulltime job in a think tank was the last thing I was expecting.

"I'm listening," I said with a straight face, as my mind spun into a future featuring me driving along Malibu Beach with a blonde supermodel next to me in a new red Lexus convertible.

"Some of our projects are unique beyond words," Delaney said. "As you can see from the décor in our lobby, you and I share an interest. I too frequent the Saturday matinees at the Old Timer Theatre, as well as other special presentations at motion-picture houses in Los Angeles. The sci-fi elements of some of those films were as amazing back when they were produced, as some of our research projects may seem today.

"To boil it down, when you are on the edge of a new technology, there is an aspect of adventure that must be met without fear. I believe you, Dave, will understand what we are doing and, perhaps, help us succeed as well as communicate our success to our governmental partners."

Wow! I thought. "So let's take a look. Show me. Tell me."

Delaney opened a file folder and spread out a few photographs on the table.

"One of our projects that will, hopefully, soon be used to help mankind is artificial human tissue that can be designated with the exact DNA of a recipient. Burn patients will be able to receive skin grafts customized so their bodies will not reject them. This is a very exciting breakthrough that we hope to make available for governmental testing within the next year."

Obviously the professor had already done quite a bit of testing from the photos he moved in front of me.

"You are cloning tissues?"

"We are creating tissues," he clarified. "Then we are designating their DNA for specific recipients. We've successfully created skin, a nose, an ear and a kidney that have been surgically transplanted to accident victims with no problems of rejection."

"That's wonderful," I said.

"It is, but it's only the tip of the iceberg. We are working on creating other organs that could be reproduced quickly enough to help every patient in need. Our idea is that large hospitals would be able to manufacture a stockpile, for lack of a better word, of hearts, livers, kidneys, etc. When a patient is deemed to need a transplant, surgeons could simply take a small blood sample to program the new organ's DNA. We hope to get that process down to a matter of hours."

"Sounds like a wonderful ability, Zack, but I am also reminded of a few classic horror films."

"In the process of achieving our current results we did go a bit too far," he said. "We thought, since we can create organs, let's try to create life. It can't be done! We can help living humans but we cannot create a new living, thinking being."

"I'm glad you failed," I said. "But since you can create parts, why do you suppose you couldn't put them together and bring them to life?"

"The same reason you can't bring a mannequin to life—no soul. Although we never see it, I believe our failure has proven the existence of the soul."

The conversation seemed quite strange coming on the heels of an afternoon of B-westerns and Betty Boop cartoons.

"But you will see some of our work in that direction soon," Delaney said. "Another of our quests has been to quantify time."

"Huh?"

"We all know about time, but does it really exist? We have a past and a future. But our present is in constant motion. There is no now."

If Delaney had been speaking to a class of college freshmen, I'd bet eyes would have glazed, mouths would have opened and at least one or two members of his audience would have torn up their medical marijuana cards. Of course, if he had been speaking in Oregon, they might've torn up their medical heroin or mushroom cards. My head felt like it was getting ready to explode.

"Don't tell me you're taking H.G. Wells seriously?"

"We've spent the last eight years debating and experimenting with time," he said. "We've come up with a few answers, anyway. Come with me."

We walked out of the conference room into another hall. This one was an express in that it didn't have any other doors along the way until it ended at an elevator.

"From the outside, your building doesn't look like it has a second floor."

"Oh, it does. We have several other floors, but they are all beneath us."

We entered the elevator, which had no buttons. The doors closed behind us, and Delaney said, "Time level, please." I could feel us descending.

The elevator stopped, doors opened and we entered a huge room that seemed like the inside of a soundstage at Universal Studios. The walls were lined with enormous mechanical apparatuses containing copper coils, meshed gears of a variety of sizes and shapes, crackling electrical arcs, tanks of boiling liquid and vibrating steel plates. In the center of the room was a very large ice structure that looked like an igloo, had it been constructed by Conrad Hilton.

"Holy Mukluk, Zack!" I said.

"It's not a Fortress of Solitude," he explained. "The ice keeps the equipment we have inside at the correct temperature and prevents all outside interference from contaminating our experiments."

I nodded my head as if I actually understood what he said.

"Shouldn't all this mechanical stuff have a control board, a large circuit breaker switch and a hunchback to pull it?" I asked.

"I can control all of that with my laptop," Zack answered as we walked toward the igloo.

CHAPTER TWO
IT'S A MATTER OF TIME

Upon entering the ice lab, everything I had seen so far became about as futuristic as a Victrola. An aqua-blue light emanating through the ice walls saturated the interior with an undersea glow. I could see a webbing of what was probably heavy duty electrical lines solidly positioned within the ice. A circle of immense, carved crystal structures pinned with cables and tubes throbbed with energy directed at a centrally positioned 20-foot-by-20-foot, stainless steel enclosure.

"Nice refrigeration," I said. "Is this where you store your meat and vegetables?"

"Close," Zack said, with a slight smirk on his face.

A sliding door opened and we entered the steel box. Surprisingly, the interior of the structure was a glass oval containing many holes and small gun-barrel-like projections pointing toward a round marble table which held a covered mass about the size of a human body. Green light filtered through the clear glass floor, illuminating everything with upwardly demonic shadows that meshed with the aqua blue lighting from the ice, culminating with an almost X-ray like glow to our skin.

There was a slight, wet-chemical smell in the air coming off of the ice that left a metallic taste in my mouth. I stared at the man-sized form on the table as a cold, damp chill ran up my back and ordered the hairs on my neck to stand at attention.

"Before you begin spouting guesses that reference Lionel Atwill, Whit Bissell or Commando Cody, I'd like to explain a few things," Zack said. "I've already mentioned that we are working on creating genetically coded human tissues. Under that cover is a complete human body, created and coded in the laboratory."

I noticed the blanket was slightly lifting as if its occupant was breathing heavily in a deep sleep.

"I thought you admitted you couldn't create life," I said.

"That's true. The body is breathing. Its heart is beating and blood is pumping. The tissues—organs, skin, hair, nerves, nails, etc.—are alive. But it is not human. It has no thoughts, no ability to control movement—no soul! The involuntary movements of the heart, lungs and system operate on automatic, like a wind-up clock."

"Cut to the chase, Zack. If you are just perfecting genetically coded transplant organs and tissues, why is this complete body here?"

Professor Zachariah Delaney pulled at his mustache and thought.

"Those experiments have worked to our advantage in relation to our studies of possible time travel," he said calmly.

I let his answer soak in a moment as I began to wonder if I was ever going to be able to climb out of this wonderland rabbit hole. I walked forward and reached toward the cloth covering the body. As I grasped the material, my mind flashed to a scene of actress Mary Philbin unmasking Lon Chaney in the 1925 classic film "Phantom of the Opera." Zack firmly took hold of my shoulder and stopped me in my tracks.

"Let's go back where it is a mite warmer," he said. "You'll have plenty of time to examine him after we discuss a few things."

My curiosity was split into two separate controlling factors. One side of me wanted to rip that blanket off the body while the other side warned me to step back and see what Zack had to say, because that could be a Christopher Lee-like beast under there, just waiting to pull its lips back from sharp fangs and leap at me. I walked back out of the ice chamber with the professor while my mind told me I needed to cut back on watching weird movies.

We returned topside to the "starship" conference room with the glass table.

"By the look on your face, I see we have garnered your interest," Zack said. "And I assure you, there is nothing to fear, just yet. And I believe you want to learn more."

"I do," I said. "Your inference is that there may be some danger in what you, we if I'm part of this, are doing."

"As with all the great sci-fi flicks we both enjoy so much, there is always danger involved with scientific advancement. The early explorers discovered new lands, but not without sacrifice. The same can be said about the Manhattan Project, our amazing space program, laparoscopic surgery, artificial sweeteners and just about every scientific discovery of the last couple of centuries.

"I believe you have the skills we need as well as an interest in futuristic possibilities that, I can honestly say, are equal to those wild speculations we both enjoy in the great Republic serials."

This guy is crazier than I am, I thought. He talks of time travel and skin grafting while he keeps a homemade non-living, but breathing human body in his ice laboratory. One side of my mind told me to stand up and run. But the side that has always led me to some of my more adventuresome, and sometimes quite stupid, actions told me to keep listening. And on that side, an image of that red Lexus convertible kept flashing through my thoughts.

"Time travel," he said. "If that can be achieved, we can only move forward in time and, hopefully, return safely. Any actions we take in the future, will not impact current reality. But, the man who goes back in time could just slightly change the activity of those in the past, and that would magnify outward—possibly changing everything we know in our present."

"Some people would like to go back to 1963 and take out Lee Harvey Oswald before he assassinated the president," I said. "And in doing so, everything that happened after November 22, 1963, would be different, to the point that the time travel project that sent the traveler back might never have been created."

"Exactly," Zack said. "That could rip the delicate webbing of time and destroy our universe."

My mouth seemed dry and my head began to ache.

"We don't know what would happen," he continued. "Whatever it is, we do not want to end reality."

"So," I said. "Your experiments will concentrate on possible travel into the future."

"Oh, no! We're going into the past. You and I are just going to be very careful about it."

Oh, crap! I thought. My Lexus fantasy vanished, replaced by the vision of an ancient, cracked tombstone with my name on it and a death date of June in

1876, during the Battle of the Little Bighorn.

"I can see you're a slight apprehensive about things," Zack said. "So, let's lighten the conversation just a little bit."

"Gladly."

"You're quite a fan of the flickers shown at the Old Timer Theatre, especially some of the great B-westerns."

"I am."

"And you also know a lot about the people who made those films. I just saw you there with your nephew enjoying the Rough Riders."

It kind of creeped me out that, according to my somewhat paranoid take on things, Sammy and I had been stalked.

"Don't let it upset you," he said. "As I told you, we chose you for this job. And, we did our due diligence in running a thorough background check, among other things, to make sure you were the right person for our scientific journey—adventure—if you would rather use that word."

"What does my interest in old Rough Riders films have to do with anything?"

"You are aware that Buck Jones was born Charles Frederick Gebhart?"

"Of course," I said. "And Tim McCoy's full name was Timothy John Fitzgerald McCoy, Hoot Gibson was Edmund Richard Gibson, Tom Mix's middle name was Hezikiah and Carole Lombard was born Jane Alice Peters. That's Hollywood."

"How much do you know about Buck Jones' death?"

"He was a victim of the Cocoanut Grove fire in 1942," I said.

"On November 28, he was found by firemen, badly burned and with damaged lungs. He was taken to the hospital where he died on November 30. There were a lot of competing stories regarding what went on inside that nightclub," Zack continued. "But, like a lot of news stories these days, the alleged 'facts' don't always ring true. What we do know is that he was found on the floor near his table."

"What does the Cocoanut Grove fire have to do with your research?"

"Let's go back to the laboratory," he said, as he stood up and led the way to the elevator.

I silently followed the mysterious professor all the way back to the ice lab and the blanket-covered breathing body.

"Go ahead and lift the blanket, Dave."

I felt like I was an uninvited guest in the city morgue. Reaching forward slowly, I lifted the blanket and pulled it back exposing the body's head. My eyes bulged out and I my body tingled as if someone had just shot me with a high-voltage Taser. I was frozen, staring at a man who I had just watched on the silver screen in a B-western from 80 years ago. The breathing body on the slab was Buck Jones.

"It's not him," Zack said. "We created that body using DNA coding. As far as the world will know, that will be the body of Buck Jones that is brought out from the Cocoanut Grove. You will take it back in time. You will arrive exactly two minutes after the fire starts. According to historic accounts, that's the time the lights went out. We know where Buck Jones was found. You will arrive, you will transfer a chip-badge from the body to the real Buck Jones and then you both will return. Firemen will find this body, burned, struggling to breathe with smoke-damaged lungs. The body will be pronounced dead two days later."

I stood there with my mouth open, looking at the professor like he was from a different planet.

"What the hell, Zack? And you don't think any of that will pinch a wrinkle in the time continuum?"

"Nope. You will arrive, transfer the chip and leave with Jones within a matter of three seconds. You won't get the chance to interact with anyone else."

"Why?"

"Best question ever," Zack said. "We have sent automatic cameras back in time for less than three seconds to snap a picture and vanish. Our DNA-cloning procedures, along with the perfect scenario of that fire allows us to do the impossible—save a man's life while not effecting any behaviors that could cause damage to today's reality."

"What about the impact on our future?" I asked. "We'd be bringing a man considered dead for 80 years into today's reality, thus causing lots of wrinkles in the future."

"Not a problem. Our future hasn't happened yet. Bringing Jones in for a landing in the present will make him part of the present just like the birth of a child or the results of an election. Our future spins off of everything that happens. Our past remains locked."

Oh, great! I thought. Is this where he says, nothing can go wrong now? I felt like I needed a handful of industrial-strength Tylenols for my throbbing head. Here we were, talking about me traveling 80 years into the past with a breathing but not quite alive human body in tow, landing in the middle of the most deadly nightclub fire in history and then returning with a cowboy film star thought dead for all that time. And I hadn't even asked how much my salary was going to be or if I got holidays off.

"I know this seems so outrageous, so extreme that you are having a hard time getting a handle on the whole concept," the professor continued. "My knowledge of your abilities, your background and your interests tell me that you are our best bet for this successful launch. For lack of a better term, you have the right stuff. Although we plan on keeping the majority of our endeavors secret, for now, you will be on an equal footing with Alan Shepard, the first American to travel in space."

I pondered his words. "What if we are successful and I am able to bring Buck Jones twenty-two years into the 21st Century? How will a man who fought Muslim rebels in the Philippines in 1907, was a full-time cowboy before becoming a stuntman for Tom Mix silent films, and a movie star in black and white silent and talkie features acclimate to the age of radical Muslim terrorists in America, self-proclaimed socialist representatives and celebrities, the Internet, smartphones, driverless cars, Red China-released pandemics, 'peaceful protesters' who loot and burn stores, and the clucking, wing-flapping, headless chickens on 'The View'?"

"We will have our work cut out for us, won't we?" Zack said. "He will certainly have to learn a lot about our history and current culture. We, on the other hand, will learn even more in the process." He handed me a piece of paper with writing on it. "And this is your salary, should you decide to join us."

My eyes spun faster than a slot machine while thoughts of that Lexus returned to push me in the right direction.

"That's a great paycheck," I said. "Will it be retroactive to 1942?"

"No."

"Just kidding. So when do we crank this machine up and head to Boston 80 years ago?"

"In less than an hour," he said. "That'll give us time to get you suited up and ready to surf time."

"I need to call J.C. and let him know I'm no longer stringing for his rag."

"Don't worry about it," Zack said. "One of our people will inform him."

As if on cue, a very pretty lady in her mid-thirties with curly blonde hair and the smile of an angel wearing a white dress and lab coat entered the room carrying a light brown tweed suit, matching tie and fedora, white shirt and black wingtips. She placed the clothing on a metal chair.

"Well, hello," I smiled. "I'm Dave Custer."

"I know," she giggled. "I'm Janine Blue. Everyone calls me Sky."

"For some reason you look familiar."

"We have met," she said, and then left the room.

Zack pointed at the tweed outfit.

"Jones will think you are a typical 1942 nightclub visitor in these clothes," the professor said. "The body is wearing the very same slightly western suit that Jones will have on."

Once I donned my time-traveling attire, Zack clipped a metal tag about the size of a credit card on my pocket.

"...YOU HAVE THE RIGHT STUFF."

"Whatever you do, don't lose this," he said. "It's your ticket home. The body has an identical chip on its pocket. As soon as you land, you're to grab the body's chip and clip it on Jones' pocket."

"Then what?"

"By transferring the second chip, you will have activated the return sequence."

"Okay. I'll only be in 1942 for a few seconds. How long will the trip there and back take?"

"We don't know. Time is another dimension. You'll be outside the rules of known physics. I'm going to depend on you to make a full report on what you see, feel or otherwise experience."

Great! I thought, again. And there's no way I can purchase last-minute flight insurance.

We entered the ice globe where Zack removed the blanket from the body. The time-travel chip was clipped to his jacket pocket.

"Give me a hand, Dave. We need to flip him face down and slide him over so there's room for you."

My throat was as dry as a Death Valley horny toad's belly. Slowly I climbed up onto the slab with my traveling companion. Clutching my fedora in my hand, I made myself comfortable on my left side, facing away from the body. With his laptop in his hands, Zack backed out of the chamber. He was still visible through the white hall of ice, standing behind a podium with his computer on top. Behind him were three people looming in the shadows. I could recognize Sky Blue's amazing curves, but the other two, although familiar, were just silhouettes.

"Zack," I hollered. "How long will this take?"

"No time at all, Dave. In fact," he motioned for the others to step up out of the shadows, "you got back fifteen minutes before you arrived for your interview."

It was a good thing I wasn't on my feet, or I would have fallen to the floor. I recognized the two people standing and watching with Sky. The taller man was Buck Jones. And I was the other guy, wearing a slightly dazed expression.

CHAPTER THREE
STRANGE CARGO

The ice crackled and flashed up like a thousand klieg lights. Colorful fireworks seemed to shoot toward me from the small barrels that thrust through the glass oval. I heard a grinding sound that increased to a roar and then went completely silent as the lights dimmed. The manufactured body and I were encased in what seemed to be a pulsating barrier of arcing energy. It looked to me like our weightless bodies were flowing through a colorful roiling sea of nothingness.

I didn't know how long we traveled. I thought, of course I can't tell how long it takes to travel through time. Duh! I really needed one of those industrial strength Tylenols.

The colors vanished. Our weightlessness ended when I felt us hit the floor. I could hear screams. The lights were out, but I could tell we had arrived at the Cocoanut Grove. Flames could be seen on the other side of the room. The black smoke had dropped to about three feet above the floor. Bodies had fallen and were being trampled in an aisle not far from the table where we landed. Then I heard a thud, as a man hit the floor next to us. He wore the same suit as the body. When he lifted himself up onto his elbows and looked me directly in the eyes, I recognized the Rough Rider star.

I ripped the chip from Zack's DNA clone and clipped it to the confused cowboy's pocket. Then, I gripped his left arm above the elbow and our environment vanished into a bright white light. Once again I floated within an arcing barrier through a colorful universe of nothing. I relaxed, while considering how smooth the trip back in time had been. Then I heard a massive explosion of sound accompanied by what looked like a large four-fingered hand slapping the outside of our barrier. We bounced within the walls while something gripped our bubble and twisted it, while tossing us in many directions.

The hand tore at the arcing perimeter until it was able to breach it and reach within. I felt it grab my chest with its long pointed fingers. I believed I was going to be ripped in half until the blinding white flash hit us. The next thing I knew, I was lying in a hospital bed looking up at the beautiful smiling face of Sky Blue.

"Well, hello again," she said, "for the first time, I might add."

"So I'm back at Sundance Laboratories?"

"Yes you are, Dave. But, you haven't arrived yet for your interview and you definitely haven't left for 1942 yet."

I noticed I was wearing a hospital gown and nothing else under the bed sheet.

"Can I have a Tylenol? Preferably with a cold beer to wash it down?"

"Sure thing," she said. Then she turned to the bed to my left. "Mr. Jones. Would you like a cold beer as well?"

"Damn straight!"

The big cowboy was also wearing a hospital gown. He looked over at me and nodded.

"Were you caught in the fire too?" he asked.

"I was only there for a few seconds. I'm Dave, by the way."

"Well, we had to be pretty lucky to get out of there, Dave. I don't know how I made it, but I'm glad to be here."

Both of us were hooked to monitors, but neither of us seemed to be damaged. We were in a typical two-person hospital room with a private restroom. Buck looked around and saw the large flat-screen television mounted on the wall facing us. It was off.

"What the hell is that?"

"That's just a television," I said, knowing he had to start learning about our world sooner or later.

"Television? Like at the World's Fair?"

"Same concept, only slightly improved."

I picked up the remote from the table between us and turned it on. The 55-inch screen immediately brightened up with a beautiful blonde news anchor from Fox News.

"Whoa! What the hell? She's gorgeous, and in Technicolor! Where's the projector?"

"No projector, Buck. That young lady used to be an attorney and is now a news anchor at Fox News Network. She is being broadcast, somewhat like a radio show, and we are seeing her live."

Buck's expression became very serious as he looked around the room and up at the monitor that flashed his blood pressure, heart rate, oxygen level and other medical information.

"Just what kind of hospital is this?"

"This is a research laboratory," I answered, as I switched off the TV. "And Prof. Zachariah Delaney has a lot to explain to you about this place and how you got here."

Sky handed us each a bottle of Amber Ale and a Tylenol, which we both gulped down within seconds.

"I believe we'd like another round, Sky," I said.

"I thought you might," she said, while reaching behind a screen and producing two more bottles.

Prof. Delaney entered the room.

"See, Dave," he said. "Nothing could go wrong. Mr. Jones, welcome. I'm Prof. Zachariah Delaney. I hope you are feeling well with no lingering problems from the fire."

"I'm fine, professor," Buck said. "I'm just a little confused with the equipment and that television thingy."

"I'll explain everything soon," Zack said. "Sky. Did you find Dave's metal tag?"

"Not yet."

"It's got to be somewhere between here and the time level," the professor said. "Oh, well. You both seem fit. So go ahead and get dressed. Sky will bring you a quick bite to eat and then I'd like you to accompany her to the laboratory. Right now, I have to go meet Dave for the first time."

"Huh?" Jones asked.

I didn't have an answer for him that made sense, so I just kept quiet. Buck's clothes were on a white metal table next to the outfit I wore to the interview. By the time we finished getting dressed, Sky returned with a tray containing two hamburgers and two more beers. We both sat down on the edges of our beds and devoured the sandwiches and, although I was beginning to get a buzz from the prior two amber ales, the beer certainly helped calm my confused mind.

So, thoughts spun in my head, right now I'm downstairs attempting to interview the professor. And yet, here I am, with cowboy star Buck Jones, back from my weird road trip to 1942. And, hey, this is good beer.

"Wow!" Buck exclaimed. "This beer is the best I've had since before Prohibition. I'm gonna have to tell Tim about this stuff."

He's talkin' about Col. Tim McCoy, my brain told me. Isn't this amazing?

Then I felt sorry for the man. He had yet to learn that eighty years had flashed by since the fire. Life in America had changed dramatically during that time. Everyone he knew was dead. His wife of twenty-seven years had died in 1996. His daughter Maxine passed in 1990. Fellow Rough Riders Tim McCoy and Raymond Hatton died in 1978 and 1971, respectively. And, I thought, maybe the professor and I had not done him a favor by saving his life.

Sky turned on the TV right as a big red "News Alert" hit the screen. Another pretty blonde, this one a former White House Press Secretary, stated, "Rioting and looting continue in Portland, Los Angeles and Chicago in the name of 'social justice.' Both white-owned and black-owned businesses were reduced to ash last night while city officials ordered police officers to stand down."

News videos of Molotov cocktail-throwing rioters destroying parked vehicles, attacking pedestrians and leaving department stores through broken windows with their arms filled with stolen goods assaulted our senses. Many of the looters wore masks and shirts adorned with violent slogans. The screen cut to angry protesters filling the streets as they advanced toward boarded up neighborhoods. Some carried signs proclaiming their justifications for violence, declaring, "America is racist!" "We demand justice!" while others were more factual with statements like "Don't vote, revolt!" and adorned with hammer and sickle emblems.

I turned the television off to keep from overloading Buck Jones' grasp on reality.

"What the hell was that?" he spat. "Where in the world are we? That's insane!"

"Yes it is. And we're in Torrance, California, Buck," I said slowly, sounding a bit like a movie psychiatrist who is about to throw his patient into the snake pit. "The year is 2022."

The movie cowboy stood up, looked me in the eye and backed away toward the wall. I was thankful for two things. One there were no windows in the room that he could throw himself out of and, two he wasn't wearing any six-guns.

Sky entered the room, smiled and said, "If you both would accompany me to the lab, Prof. Delaney will explain everything."

We entered the elevator and Sky said, "Time level, please."

When we exited, the pretty blonde lady led us into the amazing lab where we stood in the shadows and watched the professor, who was at a podium working on his laptop. We could see past him into the ice chamber and onto the circular table where I saw myself stretched out next to the cloned body, looking up with bugged eyes just as the room flashed brightly and the apparatus roared and then went silent. The chamber was empty.

Prof. Delaney turned, smiled and said, "I told you everything would be fine."

He approached us like a kindly uncle at a picnic. "Buck. I'm sure you have a million questions. And we will answer every one of them. First thing though, Sky will give you a couple of shots, vaccinations that will ensure you stay healthy. We will also provide you with historical information that will seem alien to you but, after a little while, you will accept and understand everything."

The cowboy kept a straight face while staring directly into Zack's eyes.

"Buck. As soon as you get your shots, Sky will take you to your room, as I'm sure a rest will help following an evening of celebration, the tragic fire and this confusing situation. Dave. I trust everything went smoothly."

"No, Zack, it didn't. Something happened on the way back."

"Let's go have a private debriefing," he said. "Buck's had a very long and tedious day and he needs a night's rest."

Buck looked like he was on the edge of a breakdown as Sky tried to calm him on the way out of the lab. Zack and I once more went to the starship conference room. We no sooner sat down facing each other when the door opened and Beth, the pretty brunette receptionist, brought in two bottles of amber ale.

"Here's to the first man to travel through time," he said, while holding up his bottle.

I immediately took a big swallow, thinking that although I had left 2022 first, Buck had time traveled from 1942—making him the first man to travel through time. The fact that that last sentence made sense worried me. And although the cumulative impact of the ale had certainly helped in calming my still-perplexed mental state, my concept of reality was in flux.

"Something happened during my return trip," I said.

"I take it you mean something like turbulence?"

"I mean something like some *thing*! We weren't alone on our way back to 2022. A four-fingered hand pounded on our barrier, then broke through!"

Zack remained silent.

"The hand tossed us around and tore its way into our travel bubble," I continued. "It grabbed my chest and I felt like it was trying to rip my heart out of me! All I could make out was the arm thrusting through and slamming me around, and then the bright light when we, apparently, arrived."

"I was there when you did arrive," he said. "You and Buck were alone and barely conscious. We gave you each a weak sedative to calm you down. You were only out for a short time, long enough for us to get you into our hospital room."

"So what the hell was it?"

"Tell me what you saw going in both directions."

I explained about the arcing barrier that surrounded us, and the colorful infinity that roiled outside our vessel. And I told him step by step about the strange hand that latched onto us and ripped its way through the barrier to grasp me physically.

Zack looked worried.

"What you achieved today has never been done before. You've traveled through another dimension, a universe that has never been quantified. The best-case scenario I can think of is that you were delusional and hallucinated the whole episode. The other side of the coin would be that some force, maybe not a life force that we can understand, was in the time dimension and decided to hitch a ride—maybe into our reality."

"What would that be?"

"Who knows? We don't have a clue if it needs the life-sustaining elements of our world or not to survive. We don't know if it can become a solid being here on Earth or if it is a traveling invisible creature that has no way to make its existence known. Perhaps it's spiritual or a sprite-like force such as luck or even evil."

It didn't seem like the professor had a handle on the situation. That was unnerving, I thought, but it could be nothing. The alien world of the time dimension may have just played a number on my mind and caused me to hallucinate the whole thing. I wasn't going to worry about it as, with all the unknowns we faced in acclimating Buck Jones into the new century, we had plenty on our plates.

Zack showed me to my apartment, where I took the time to freshen up and then take a four-hour nap. It was a fairly nice modern space with a living/dining area and separate bedroom like one would get in a five-star hotel. I could get used to this, I thought to myself. And yet, I decided I would also keep my little bungalow within walking distance of Redondo Beach.

Hell, I thought. I can afford it.

Following my nap, I called the facility operator, who turned out to be a robot voice, and she got Zack on the line. I asked him what I should do next. He said that Buck just couldn't sleep, so Sky had already started his modern history lessons. Zack and I decided to check in to see how Sky was doing in bringing Buck up to speed on his situation. When we entered his apartment, the cowboy star was seated in a plush recliner while watching black and white newsreel footage on a big-screen television. Sky sat in a wingback chair, the remote in her hand as she was able to slow down, back up or stop the action to further explain the films.

"We prepared these videos over a period of three years, just in case our experiments were successful," Zack said.

"Buck had a hard time with the Cocoanut Grove fire footage," Sky said. "But he is now doing his best to understand. The current films are catching him up on 1944."

"You're telling me America and our allies won this World War in 1945?" Jones said. "I'm going to have a million questions just regarding the war."

"We have a whole lot of research materials in our facility library," Zack said. "Once you get through as much of the video material as you can stand, you may want to spend a few weeks in the library to acclimate yourself into the 21st Century."

"So there's been a lot of water under the bridge since the Rough Riders," Buck said. "Do you think I'm forgotten enough so that I could just walk out onto the streets in 2022?"

"You're not recognizable to a lot of people today," the professor answered. "But there are quite a few folks out there, like Dave and me, who are fans of classic westerns. In 1960, the Hollywood Chamber of Commerce honored you with a star on the Hollywood Boulevard Walk of Fame. In fact, there are television channels that only broadcast the great westerns of the past, including yours. So, because of that, we will create a new identification for you."

"How about I just go back to Charlie Gebhart?"

"Too close," I said. "Someone like me who loves the Rough Rider movies and knows your real name might get suspicious. After all, we're not going to change how you look."

"How about Buck Roberts?"

"Once again, you used that name in too many of your movies."

"Charlie Roberts?"

"That could work," Zack said. "We'll prepare your identification."

Buck looked into Zack's eyes and asked, "Why? What good am I going to be? What's my value to this bizarre Brick Bradford world?"

"Your first-hand knowledge of the early 20th Century is priceless," Zack said. "Because of our excursion to 1942 and back, we will be learning amazing things for years to come. And together, since you are now part of the Sundance team, we will achieve scientific discoveries that will make today's advancements seem like the first horseless carriages."

"And what will I be doing right away?"

"You'll continue your lessons with Sky and probably spend a lot of time with Dave over the next few weeks."

"What about the other guy?" Jones asked.

"What other guy?" Zack said.

"The other guy that seemed to be jumbling around with us as you brought me out of the fire?"

The professor and I looked at each other, then back at Buck.

"Describe him," I said.

"He was just a blur," Jones explained. "It was like we were in a bag floating in white-water rapids. The other guy seemed to crawl into the bag and wrap himself around you. I couldn't tell if he was wearing a white suit or robe, but he had long fingers and black eyes."

CHAPTER FOUR
OLD FRIENDS AND NEW

It was a crisp cool sunrise when I hopped into my Ford Fiesta and drove toward Redondo Beach. The last several hours had seemed like, well, several hours. I needed to get to my bungalow and take stock of my environment, my life to that point, and do what I could to digest what I had gone through and what was going to happen next.

Parking was, as usual, difficult. I ended up having a three-block walk to my home. A notion flashed through my mind that, perhaps, my fantasy Lexus wouldn't be safe parked on the streets in my neighborhood. I thought, at least my Fiesta was secure as no one was stupid enough to steal one of those.

I don't know why I seemed surprised when I entered my home and found that nothing had changed. There were dishes in the sink. An empty pizza box leaned against my kitchen trash container. A half-full bottle of stale beer stood on my coffee table and my closet door was open in the bedroom where I was able to grab a clean pair of jeans and a shirt. I placed them on my unmade bed and added clean socks and shorts to the pile.

I got undressed and tossed my dirty clothes into an overflowing hamper on my way to the shower. It took about three minutes for the water to warm up. Then I was able to stand in the therapeutic flow and wash the prior day's grime, as well as some 1942 Cocoanut Grove soot, from my body. I had thought a warm shower would have calmed my worried brain, but it didn't. One doesn't go through the type of strangeness I had and come away unscathed. It would take time.

I stepped out of the shower and in front of the mirror, trying to see if my appearance had changed in any way.

"You feeling better?" my reflection asked.

"A little—Wha…?"

"Hi, Dave. Thanks for the ride into 2022," my mirror image said, using one of my dumbest smiles.

I grabbed the sink for support, as my knees felt like rubber bands.

"Be careful," it said. "Every year, close to 235,000 accidents take place in bathrooms. That floor is quite hard."

"What in the hell is…?"

"I got that stat from your Internet," it said. "Once I got here, your Internet was the first trip I took. It was slightly confusing in that history seems to be a work of fiction to many of the websites. And quite a few of the other sites I visited were just plain sick!"

"No, no, no, no…" I stammered.

"Move your lips, Dave," the image said, sounding a bit like Rex Harrison. "Take a deep breath and enunciate. Repeat after me. My plane in Maine is kept in a hangar in Bangor."

"What the hell are you?" I screamed.

"A good question. Let's just say I'm a happy wanderer, joyous minstrel, mirthful raconteur and delightful companion throughout the ages."

"You attacked me on my way back from 1942!"

"No, Dave. I just hopped a ride in your carriage a bit like Jimmie Rodgers on a flatcar. I did no harm."

Once again my mind was spinning like I had dropped down into Disney's animated Wonderland only to find myself inside that giant tomato worm's bong. I ran out of the bathroom and got dressed, even though I was still quite wet.

Crap! Crap! Crap! I thought, while pulling on my western boots. I was having a worse time trying to adapt to my alleged reality than Buck Jones, who had just arrived from eighty years ago.

I stuck my head back into the bathroom, looked into the mirror and my jaw dropped as I smiled back at me and waved. Crap! Crap! Crap!

"How long are you gonna haunt my mirror?" I hollered.

"Oh, is that distressing? I just thought it would be an easy way to introduce myself and say hello. Sorry."

He faded and was replaced by my real, bug-eyed image. Thank God! I thought. I hoped he had traveled on to someone else's madness. I turned and walked back to the living room and switched on my classic 1939 Crosley radio. I had it tuned to a 30s station, which inundated the room with the amazing harmonious scatting of the Boswell Sisters. I turned to plop myself into my La-Z-Boy recliner so I could purge my brain of, oh, just about everything, when I realized someone was already occupying it. I reached back and turned off the radio.

Dressed in coveralls and a railroad worker's hat, the Singing Brakeman Jimmie Rodgers sat in my recliner strumming a guitar. He did a perfect "Yodeling Cowboy," as I stood motionless with my jaw hanging low. He finished the song, smiled and waited for applause.

"What the…?"

"You're not gonna start that again, are you?"

"Jimmie Rodgers?"

"A great guy," he said. "I was there when he recorded that song. That boy was the sound of the working people. Not many have equaled him since."

"Are you going to go around haunting people disguised as yodeling singers?"

"Oh, God no. Most folks can't see me."

Okay. So I now have a new, high-paying, fulltime job, I thought. I will be working with a cowboy movie star everyone thought died eighty years ago. And, I'm being haunted by a strange being who can shape-shift and yodel, except no one else can see him.

I took a deep breath. "So what do I call you?"

"I think I should have a modern name this time," he said. "I've been Hieronymus, Wyatt, Ulysses, Bob and Raymond. But I want a 21st Century name."

"Bob is pretty much a today name."

"Mine was short for Bobulinski. Nobody uses that one any more."

"What about Raymond?"

"I got tired of that one back in the colonies. It was popular though. Everybody loved Raymond."

My mind was telling me the yodeling dick-weasel was just messing with me.

"Do you want a beer?" I asked, because I really needed one.

He nodded and I brought two cans into the room and handed him one.

"Lucky Lager," he smiled. "That's it. Call me Lucky!"

"Okay, Lucky. So what's the deal? You're invisible to everyone else but me. Why?"

"Because I used you, and your chariot to get here. We spectrally bonded," he answered. "So, since it does get lonely wandering around invisible to the local life forms, I'm just gonna tag along with you a while. I can be a help to you, in that I'm really quite smart. And for the good news, your friend who was also in the chariot will probably be able to see me as well."

"My friend is Buck Jones."

"Oh, my. He was a darn good cowboy."

"Still is," I said. "As for smart, I guess if you can absorb the Internet information this quickly, you do have a leg up on the rest of us."

"Your Internet is not all that honest or reliable," he said. "It looks to me that much of history has been rewritten by either very stupid or very Machiavellian people. I visited this world many times, and I'm emphasizing the word 'times.' And I've personally attended a lot of real historic events."

"Like…"

"Like scientific discoveries, leaders and their decisions, wars, Bergen and McCarthy radio broadcasts, just about everything your Internet and history books fail to report accurately."

"You drink beer. Do you eat?"

"Of course. But anything I drink or eat will vanish as it goes in my mouth, so no one sees any embarrassing visuals. And, if I pass gas, the closest person will have to take the blame."

He laughed. I didn't quite understand why until we had lunch together later that day at my favorite diner. That's when I discovered he had some kind of really weird alien metabolism, with an even weirder sense of humor!

"Back to my original question," I said. "Are you an extraterrestrial being, a supernatural specter or some kind of a mythological wraith?"

"Yes and no," he said. "There are an infinite number of universes, with unique physical properties. Also, the time dimension is only one of many concepts outside your world's understanding. I'm just a traveler who has landed here on your world for a visit, again, and I'm not looking to cause any problems."

As my mind danced along in a conga line of insanity, I realized that Buck Jones really didn't need one more bit of craziness to be thrust on him. The poor man was probably going to collapse into the fetal position the first time he experienced downtown freeway traffic, I surmised. And now I was going to have to explain to him that the weirdo with me was invisible to everyone else and personally knew many figures from history. Piece of cake, I thought. Yeah, broccoli, bamboo and Wuhan bat cake.

We went to the aforementioned diner and I ordered a burger, fries and a side of onion rings. The invisible being seated across from me in the booth was able to swipe most of the onion rings and fries. I gripped my hands tightly around my burger. I had to have two refills on my diet Pepsi, thanks to the yodeling spirit.

There weren't any diners seated around us, so we could converse quietly.

"So. Lucky. What can you tell me about the future?"

"Nothing. I haven't been there. My visits have all just been sort of now and then trips."

"Huh?"

"Now and then. I always visit during the present, like 'now.' I've done that quite a few times, as times pass, thus they became 'then.' Understand?"

"Not really. When was your first visit?"

"Oh, that was a doozy. I popped in on a hunting party that was battling another tribe over the rights to a large hairy elephant with long tusks."

"A mastodon?"

"That's not what they called it. Anyway, as luck would have it, no members of either group could see me. So I was able to dine with the winners without them knowing it, which was a good thing. They were serving a combo-plate of elephant and loser meat."

"How're the fries?" I asked, as I decided I really didn't need the last third of my burger.

Lucky looked at me with a very weird expression on his Jimmie Rodgers face. Then it hit me. He had passed the most disgusting, horrible, evil gas this side of a skunk-town sewer plant. I jumped to my feet, grabbed the bill and ran to the cash register so I could pay up and get out. I really wanted to be away from the building when the waitress came by to clean the table.

We climbed into my Fiesta for the drive back to Sundance Laboratories, which baffled a young woman who was walking her sweater-wearing dog when she saw my passenger door apparently open and close by itself. She bent low and looked at me with question marks in her eyes through my driver's side window, which was open.

"The door?" I said. "Oh, that's just a computer glitch. I asked Alexa and she told me not to worry about it. But then again, she's the same gigabyte girl who holds my radio on polka music."

I smiled and drove away.

"The dog-lady seemed confused," Lucky said.

"There's a lot of that goin' around."

Lucky was still wearing his Jimmie Rodgers railroad disguise when we arrived at the lab. Once inside, the receptionist announced me before we got to her desk. "Hi, Dave. Zack will meet you in the conference room."

I led the way with the invisible singing brakeman trailing behind. We sat down across from each other at the Starship Enterprise table. Lucky held a guitar in his lap.

"Where the hell did you get that guitar?" I asked. "You didn't have it in my car."

"We wandering minstrels have little tricks that keep our performances fresh," he said. "I'm never without my guitar. It's just not always in solid form."

This guy is gonna drive me nuts, I thought. Then Zack, Buck and Sky walked in.

"You look refreshed," Zack said. "And, you'll be glad to know that Buck is assimilating our history lessons quite well. He seems resigned to the reality of the situation and is adjusting at light speed."

"That's great," I said. "But we have a new wrinkle to iron out."

Sky went to a small refrigerator under a counter and brought back four beers.

"We'll need one more," I said, as she and Zack looked confused.

Buck shook his head and stared at Lucky. "So, Jimmie. Did they go get you too?"

"What's happening?" Zack asked.

Then Lucky strummed his guitar and started to sing, "T for Texas," his "Blue Yodel No. 1."

"Where's that coming from?" Sky gasped.

Buck turned toward her. "Right in front of you! That's Jimmie Rodgers!"

Zack locked eyes with me as I said, "That's the wrinkle."

Once I could get everyone to sit down, I began my slightly confused and rambling explanation of, and introduction to, Lucky. During that time, Buck, who was probably totally saturated with the surprises of his strange modern surroundings, leaned back and lit up cigar. I believed the person having the hardest time accepting the bizarre reality was the brilliant scientist professor. About halfway through my uncomfortable oration, Lucky leaned his guitar against the table and it vanished. Minstrel trick, my ass, I thought.

"So, Mr. Lucky..." Zack started to say.

"Just Lucky."

"Dave and Buck can see you but Sky and I cannot? Yet all of us can hear you?"

"That's true, whenever I want you to," Lucky answered.

"Can you walk through walls?" Sky asked.

"No."

"Can you fly?"

"Not in these clothes."

"But you can change your image to anything you want?"

"Yes," he said. "But that's not really a comic-book-worthy power if there are only two of you who can see me."

"Good point," Zack entered the conversation. "But can you change your voice to sound like just about anyone?"

Lucky answered in Zack's own voice, "Yes I can. And I can do it in all major languages from your world." Then he babbled a bit in Russian, Greek and two others that very easily could have been Vulcan and Klingon.

Zack stroked his beard and thought, while Sky went to get the invisible voice a cold beer.

"You might want to bring Buck and me another round, as well," I said.

"I'm looking forward to having some interesting conversations with you, Lucky," Zack said. "And I also think that, if you really are friendly and up to enjoying your visit to our time, you could be of great assistance to our scientific endeavors."

"Well, well, well," Lucky said, sounding a bit like Bob Crosby in front of his Bob-Cats. "I do believe we'll all just get along like a passel of pickled 'possums. And I'm always willin' to put my feet up and trade stories with my friends. Especially friends who buy the beer."

"Excuse me, Lucky," Buck said. "But I knew Jimmie Rodgers personally and I really liked his music. But it's a bit unnerving, along with everything else, just seeing him here when I did attended his funeral."

"Sorry Buck. How's this?"

Lucky morphed into Tim McCoy.

"No! That's also creepy."

"Perhaps this one," our time-hopping minstrel said, while turning into Gabby Hayes.

"Can you just be someone that I didn't know? Maybe an innocuous-looking Harold Lloyd type guy."

"Certainly, Buck."

The impish wraith immediately formed into a curly haired young man in an ill-fitting suit, bowtie and heavy-framed glasses, holding a guitar. He

"JUST LUCKY."

strummed it and began belting out "Maybe Baby."

"That's some strange music," Buck said, "but at least you're not somebody important."

Lucky, as Buddy Holly, continued his song to the end and then took a bow.

"I think I know what you did," Zack said.

"And you'd be right," I added. "But why not? Buck wasn't around for the fifties. And, I like the music."

"You guys are lucky he didn't choose MC Hammer or Vanilla Ice," Sky said. "Or even Garfunkel."

Buck remained stoic while Lucky and I chuckled.

"Thank God for small blessings," Zack said.

"So when can I get out of this building and get a look at this brave, new world?" Buck asked.

"How about this afternoon?" Zack said, surprising both Sky and me. "Lucky. I'm looking forward to some one-on-one conversations. But for right now, Buck needs a dose of 2022 reality. So, here's a plan. Dave, you and Sky take Buck and Lucky out for dinner and a movie. I suggest you go to the Retro Theatre on Vermont. Tonight's presentations are 'Outlaws of the Desert' with Hoppy, 'Death Valley Rangers' with Ken Maynard, Hoot Gibson and Bob Steel, Chapter 1 of 'Buck Rogers' with Buster Crabbe, and at least one cartoon."

I grinned at Sky, who seemed non-committal.

"That's not too far from the Burger Basket on Crenshaw," I said. "They're always busy and our invisible diner will probably not be noticed."

"Good choice," Zack said. "Now remember, Buck is Charlie Roberts." The professor handed Buck a Dodgers baseball cap. "Even a revival theatre audience couldn't recognize you without your big Stetson."

"I always did like that Brooklyn team," Buck said.

Sky leaned in and whispered in his ear.

"Los Angeles!" he exclaimed. "What the hell has happened to this country?"

"You ain't seen nothin' yet," I added.

CHAPTER FIVE
DINNER AND A MOVIE

I placed Buck Jones in the front passenger seat, where he held on tightly as I made my way down Redondo to the Harbor Freeway and then traveled about five miles until I could get off and find parking near the Burger Basket on Crenshaw. His eyes were wide and he really didn't recognize any of the areas we drove through.

Sky had left her lab jacket behind and changed into a light blue blouse and black slacks that flattered her curves. It being a rather warm southern California December, none of us needed jackets. Sky and Lucky sat in the back. And although he was invisible to her, the two of them carried on a continual conversation until we parked.

"If you like burgers and beer, you're gonna love the Burger Basket," I said. "Have you ever been here before, Sky?"

"No, Dave. This is a new treat for me."

I didn't know if she meant it or if she was handing me a line.

My three passengers found chairs at a heavy-wood table sporting a large "5" etched in the middle. I went to the counter and order four "specials," which contained cheeseburgers and fries, and four bottles of amber ale. When I returned, Sky was showing Buck photographs on her iPhone. I couldn't tell if the old cowboy understood her, or if he believed he needed a silver cross to ward off her witchcraft.

The Burger Basket was doing a swell business, as most of the tables were full and several folks were seated at the bar. The jukebox was playing a classic Merle Haggard song loud enough to be heard over the raucous conversations of celebrating diners. A large group of middle-aged women in big silly red hats were having a very good time at a long table not far from us. Whatever they were talking about must have been hilarious, as they punctuated their continual laughing with outbursts of excessive laughing. Whatever floats your boat, I thought.

"The food must be good," Buck said. "This place seems to be quite popular, a bit like Philippe's on Aliso Street."

"That's on Alameda now," I said. "And it's still popular."

A waiter delivered the four baskets and beers to our table. He looked at the "empty" chair.

"That's for our friend," Sky said. "He'll be along any minute."

The burgers tasted great and the ale was to die for. While we ate, conversed and enjoyed ourselves, as if on cue, a large man in a black T-shirt, Levis and wearing a red bandana on his unkempt, thinning hair, came to our table and grabbed the back of the "empty" chair.

"Takin' the chair," he said.

"That chair is already taken," Buck stated.

"It's taken alright," the surly man said. "'Cause I'm takin' it!"

He turned to walk away, yanking the chair as he went. The "empty" chair didn't move because of the weight of the invisible minstrel sitting in it, and the bandana-wearing Bozo's feet went out from under him, dropping him on his butt. Our table, as well as several close by, got a good laugh out of that.

"What are you tryin' to pull!" the chair thief screamed as he got to his feet.

Buck stood up in front of the man and said, "You were just mistaken in thinking the chair was not occupied, Greasy. Our friend is coming back. You, on the other hand, are going away."

The unruly rascal yanked his right arm back to throw a punch. Buck brought his left hand up and buried his fist in the man's solar plexus, leading to a loud exhale, and allowing him to plant a right hook into the man's left cheek and eye. Greasy dropped to the floor gasping for air.

Two other miscreants, who seemed to be friends of the chair thief, hurried toward our table. Unfortunately for them, they couldn't see Buddy Holly as he rushed over and tripped the second man into the first. The first man rolled over to get to his feet while his friend reached down to help him. Lucky smacked the man on the floor, who, thinking his friend hit him, struggled to stand up while cursing.

"What the hell's the matter with you, asshole?" he screamed. "You hit me again and I'll rip your head off and throw it through the window!"

"I didn't hit you!"

They stood face-to-face and glowered at each other. Lucky shoved the second man from behind into the first guy. Then the fists began to fly. Lucky returned to our table and had a swig of his beer. "What's eatin' those guys?"

Buck grabbed the chair thief by his feet and dragged him out the door. Within a moment, he came back, grinned and took a big bite of burger. "I found him a comfortable spot in a dumpster."

A few members of the staff were trying to separate the other two men when a couple of police officers arrived, thumped one of the aggressors over the head with a club and cuffed them both. As the lawmen marched the rowdy duo past us, Sky said, "Thank you, officers. Those men were behaving like maniacs."

The younger of the two policemen smiled and said, "You're very welcome, miss."

"And thank you, Lucky," I said. "You and Buck are quite a team."

"Well, that's one thing that hasn't changed in eighty years," Buck said. "Just about anywhere you go, there's always a couple of jerks lookin' to get their butts kicked."

"Make that a lot more than eighty years, Buck," Lucky added.

We finished our meal and climbed back in my car to drive just a few blocks to the Retro Theatre on Vermont. Buck looked up at the marquee and said, "This is goin' to be interesting."

I have to say that I agreed. The two oaters, serial chapter and cartoon were right up my alley. Sky, however, looked like she might nod off after the first fifteen minutes. I bought three tickets and we entered close together, with our invisible friend along for the ride.

"You up for popcorn?" I asked Sky.

"No, thank you. I'm just hopin' I can keep awake."

"Sit next to me."

She looked at me out of the corner of her eye. "That might just do it."

The Retro was a fairly small theatre that catered to classic-movie enthusiasts. And, even though TCM and other channels offered television viewers a wide assortment of old movies and TV shows, many of us still appreciated seeing the films on the big screens.

About half of the seats were filled for the western double feature presentation. We chose four on the aisle and made ourselves comfortable. Sky and I sat together while Buck sat on the other side of our "empty" seat.

Projected trivia slides were asking classic-film questions prior to the first feature. Two rather obnoxious teenage boys sat across the aisle a few rows away from us, loudly answering the questions with wrong and somewhat rude responses while laughing at their own attempts to be funny.

"If those two dopes continue gasbagging when the movie starts, I'm gonna box 'em on the ears," Buck whispered.

"Not a problem," Lucky said. "I got this one."

Buck and I watched as Lucky got up and meandered over to sit right behind the two young loudmouths. He turned toward us with an extremely silly smile on his face. Then he got up and came back. The two boys suddenly stopped their mouthy routine and looked at each other with total disgust in their eyes.

"What the hell?" one of them said loudly, as he stood up and stepped into the aisle.

"Jeeze! What crawled up your butt and died?" the other one hollered. "Holy, crap!"

Then several other people a few rows away stood up and moved out of their seats and farther from the two offensive youths. "Oh, my God!" One woman held her hand over her mouth and nose as she scurried to another part of the auditorium. "You should be ashamed!" she yelled at the two boys.

"They wanted to be the center of attention," Lucky said, as he sat back down next to us. "Now they really are."

Hearing the rather loud complaints, an usher rushed to the two offenders, slapped his hand over his mouth and nose and exclaimed, "Good God!" He then started shining his flashlight on the seats and floor where they had been sitting. Many outraged audience members pointed at the youths as they both hurried out of the auditorium.

I looked at Lucky and shook my head.

"Hey! I got the job done. Nobody's ears were boxed. I just used one of my many super powers."

"Just don't do a repeat performance over here," Buck said.

"No problem."

The audience quieted down as the lights lowered and the Trail Blazers feature came on. Monogram Pictures had launched the Trail Blazers in 1943 with Ken Maynard, Hoot Gibson and Bob Steel to fill the void from the loss of the Rough Riders series. And, although the three veteran movie cowboys did a fine job of takin' care of the screen villains, their series never reached the popularity of the Jones, McCoy, Hatton films.

About halfway through the oater I noticed Sky had fallen asleep. I decided not to wake her up, since her beautiful blonde head was resting on my shoulder. I even forgave her for being bored by the B-western film, in that her closeness had definitely improved my movie-watching experience.

The film concluded and the lights came on for a short intermission. Sky opened her eyes, looked up at me and awkwardly excused herself to use the ladies' room.

"I'll be right back," Lucky said, as he got up and followed Sky.

"I'm glad I don't need to go to the men's room," I said. "I have a feeling Lucky might cause a bit of a flap in there."

"Better there than here," Buck said, then changed the subject. "That was an interesting flicker with Ken and Hoot. They both were a bit longer in the tooth than when I saw them last. Especially Ken."

"Yeah," I said. "Maynard was older, heavier and, according to historical accounts, a bit surlier by the time the Trail Blazers came along. He was only in a few of them before he bailed."

"Ken always did have a problem with the bottle," Buck said. "He also had a bit of a temper."

"It was a shame too, in that he was loved by western fans," I said. "In fact, when television came along and all those westerns were used to fill broadcast time, kids of the 1950s became big fans. All of the westerns of the 1930s and '40s were new again in the early days of TV."

"Both Ken and Hoot were amazing horsemen who could do their own stunts back in the silent and early talkie days," Buck recalled. "But this film, well, Monogram didn't even try to get stuntmen who were the same size as the aging stars. In one scene, we see six-foot-plus tall Maynard reach up to climb a building. Then they cut to the stuntman, probably five-foot-six Harvey Parry in a black cowboy outfit and giant white hat, scurrying up the side of the structure and running across the roof."

"It was kind of obvious, wasn't it?" I said. "But, one has to overlook a lot to enjoy a good low-budget western."

"It sure looked like you enjoyed it," he added, "once Sky fell asleep on your shoulder."

"That was nice."

"You know, Dave. With all the amazing 21st Century shit being thrown at me, I've been doin' my best to adapt while keeping sane. But my mind keeps telling me that Dell and Maxine are gone. In fact, most, if not all, of the young fans that attended my films on Saturday afternoons are all dead as well. My time is over. I really don't belong here."

I didn't know what to say. The America he grew up in, fought for during his military service, supported with War Bond drives, and depicted in his films no longer existed. All of his family and friends were dead. And I certainly didn't have the heart to tell him that there hadn't been a decent western film produced in almost thirty years (the last being Clint Eastwood's amazing "Unforgiven").

A white-haired older gentleman wearing a Cubs baseball cap and a khaki jacket stepped in front of me.

"Excuse me," he said. "I've seen you at the Old Timer Theatre in Long Beach, several times."

I put out my hand and shook his. "I'm Dave. And yep, I attend the Saturday matinees there quite often."

"I'm Ben," he said. "And I'm the last of the South Bay Hoppy Fan Club members."

"There are still a lot of us who enjoy those films," I said.

"Well, I'm always glad to meet another B-western aficionado," he added. "And I give out these coins to people who are true western fans."

He held out a coin and placed it in my hand. It was an old Hopalong Cassidy Lucky Coin.

"Wow! This is great, Ben. But…"

"Don't worry," he said. "I have several left. I only give them to people who I know will appreciate them."

He then turned and walked away. I placed the coin inside my wallet for safekeeping.

Sky smiled and sat down next to me. "I could hear a bit of a squabble coming from the men's room," she said. "I hope there isn't a problem."

Then a grinning Lucky returned and sat down in the "empty" seat.

"I think I know what the problem was," I told Sky. "And I'm sure it's over now. Nothing to worry about."

The lights dimmed and Chapter 1 of "Buck Rogers," with Buster Crabbe, crackled onto the screen. As with all of the great serials, the amazing action began in the first few minutes, with Rogers and his sidekick flying a dirigible over the North Pole during a destructive storm. I love this stuff, I thought. Then I looked down at Sky's curls and smiled as she snuggled into my shoulder and began to snore like a kitten. I *really* love this stuff!

As the adventure hit the point where the audience just knew there was not going to be any way the hero could have survived, the titles told us to not miss "Chapter 2, Tragedy on Saturn. Next week in this theatre."

"We better get Miss Blue home," I said. "She's all tuckered out."

"I've seen the Hoppy flick before, anyway," Buck added.

The screen flashed a couple of times and a Scrappy cartoon began as we made our way out of the auditorium.

While we walked through the lobby and out the theatre door, a loud "Yeehaw!" alerted us. A towheaded boy of about seven ran out the door with his mother attempting to keep up with him.

"At least some kids still love the classic westerns," I said.

The child, who moved faster than a cartoon roadrunner, ran in circles under the marquee while pointing his index fingers into the air and pretending to fire his imaginary six-guns.

"Calm down, Jimmy!" his mother hollered as she tried to capture the boy.

Jimmy, probably blowing off a little snack-bar-sugar energy, laughed and ran off the edge of the sidewalk and directly out into the Vermont Avenue traffic, as his mother yelled "No!"

With the speed of his legendary quick-draw, Buck Jones took one step, reached out and yanked Jimmy back to the sidewalk just as a speeding Subaru roared by. Things happened so fast that everyone in front of the theatre stood motionless as the big cowboy wearing a Dodgers cap handed the confused boy to his frightened and grateful mother. She dropped to one knee and hugged her son. "Thank God! Thank God!" she said. "And thank you, sir."

"You're very welcome, ma'am," Buck said. "Better hold tight to this little critter for a while. He's champin' at the bit."

The four of us walked toward my Fiesta.

"You know, Buck," I said. "You told me you didn't think you belonged here. Well. If you weren't here tonight, that young man wouldn't currently be safe in his mother's arms."

We quietly climbed into my car and pulled out into the traffic. I believed Buck was probably beginning to understand that life wasn't going to be the same as he had been used to, but that it was still precious.

"That was fun," Lucky stated. "My question now is, just where am I gonna stay the night?"

"Let's just get back to the lab," I said. "Buck and I have apartments there.

Lucky, I'll fix you up with a couple of blankets and you can crash in the recliner. Sky. Do you have a room at the lab?"

"No. But my car is there and I can drive home."

"As tired as you seem, I think it would be a lot safer if you just slept in my bed."

"Safer for whom?"

"I mean, I can curl up on the couch and you can have the whole bedroom," I quickly stammered.

"That sounds good," she chuckled. "I'm sure Zack will have work for all of us in the morning. And I do keep clean clothes and an overnight kit in my locker."

"So you've worked quite a few long-hour days," I stated.

"You've seen some of the amazing scientific breakthroughs the professor has made," she explained. "That doesn't happen by working eight to five."

"From what I've seen, you've accomplished a tremendous amount," I stated. "But why aren't there more people at the labs?"

"Sundance is a think tank that focuses primarily on the genius of Prof. Delaney," Sky responded. "We have subsidiary companies that deliver items we need, keep the facility clean and service various special requests. But, beyond that, it's just Zack, me and Beth, and now you guys, who make up the Sundance team. You three are here because of Zack's breakthrough in the time-travel project. And that increases our workload and justifies the additional staff."

We arrived at Sundance Labs and made our way to Buck's apartment.

"I've been thinkin' a bit," Jones said, while standing in the door. "The plot of that Buster Crabbe serial, as well as the comic strip on which it's based, does seem somewhat familiar."

"What are the odds?" Lucky asked.

Sky showed Lucky and me to the locker room where she retrieved a clean blouse, skirt, underclothes and a small overnight kit and placed them in a carpetbag. "This should do me fine," she said.

"What about nightclothes?" I asked.

"Don't get personal."

My mind took a quick turn toward where it really shouldn't have as we walked back to my apartment.

"I got dibs on the bathroom," Sky announced.

We didn't argue. But I did look over at Lucky, who had sat down in the recliner, and realized I had better be second.

"Oh, and Lucky," she said, while looking around the room. "Wherever you are, keep your invisible ass out of the bedroom!"

The Buddy Holly ham began to sing "Maybe Baby," before I cut him off by throwing a pillow and blanket on top of him.

Once we had all used the bathroom, curled up in our blankets and prepared for a night's sleep, Lucky decided to get talkative.

"So, Dave," he started. "You seem to have effortlessly accepted your role in this little not-quite-existential drama. That's a bit unique for your modern culture."

"I admit I'm somewhat pragmatic."

"In earlier cultures, people believed in dragons, banshees, spirits and unique beings that today are considered myths and legends. Your American indigenous peoples had very close relationships with tribal spirits. But your generation doesn't seem to believe in anything they can't see, feel or purchase."

"As far as I know, I'm the only person of my generation to have traveled through time," I said. "That does open one's perspective to a variety of possibilities."

"Well, I congratulate you on your calm demeanor in the face of something new."

"Thanks, Lucky. What about the dragons, banshees and spirits? Were they just in earlier people's imaginations or did they exist?"

"Oh, they're real. It's just that modern cultures aren't looking for them."

Great! I thought. Now I'm gonna have to keep one eye peeled for fire-breathing lizards, screaming ghouls and tribal spooks. And on that note, I drifted off into a dream-filled sleep.

CHAPTER SIX
SEEING IS BELIEVING

"**O**utta that sack, slacker!" Sky said, as she yanked the pillow out from under my head. "Breakfast awaits."

"Blargh!" I'm usually a tad uncommunicative before my first cup of coffee. "Flleagha!"

My one open red eye saw the vision of beauty standing in front of me wearing an angel costume, which blurred a moment and turned into a lovely light-blue blouse and skirt. And although she didn't need any, she had already applied her makeup. I reached out from under the blanket and wiped away a little saliva that had trickled out of the corner of my mouth and attempted to smile.

"Everyone else is waiting at the table in Buck's apartment," she said. "We've got bacon and eggs, toast and coffee. So get your ass in the bathroom and get presentable! Your attendance is required."

She turned and marched out of the room. I noticed Lucky had folded his blanket and stacked it with his pillow on the chair. The door was open to the bedroom, where Sky had obviously made the bed. I staggered to the bathroom and threw water in my face. Then I double-checked the mirror to make sure it was really my image being reflected back at me before I started my morning ritual.

Once I was dressed and somewhat presentable, I staggered to Buck's room.

"Good morning, Mr. Custer," Lucky said. "You know, the last time I said that, things didn't turn out so well."

"Very funny," I slurred on my way to the coffee.

"Actually, there *is* a very funny story about that. It seems…"

"Later, Lucky," Buck said. "Let Dave have a cup or two of java so he can tune to the same station as the rest of us."

Zack leaned toward the "empty" breakfast chair and whispered, "And I really would like to hear that story."

I guzzled my first cup while staring at the two slices of bacon and three eggs on my plate.

"So professor," Buck said. "What's next? Are we blasting off for the moon to battle an evil emperor? Do we get our strap-on rocket packs so we can fly to Germany and destroy another dictator?"

"Actually, Buck," Zack said while spreading marmalade on his toast. "I thought we'd all go on a little vacation to a dude ranch in Arizona. I figured we could use some R and R and you might want to cowboy up a little."

All of us silently stared at the professor, who had just said the last thing we expected.

"No more time travel?" I asked.

"Not in the near future," Zack answered. "We have a lot of things to learn from your recent trip. So we're going to go through a little decompression vacation, during which all of us will share knowledge and insight. And, Buck will get more time to acclimate himself to our frenetic new world."

Jones held up a copy of the *Los Angeles Times* and said, "Frenetic doesn't quite cover it. I would use the word 'insane.' Most of today's front page is coverage on a downtown riot. The last few nights, crazy people have gathered in the streets to throw rocks, Molotov cocktails and bags of shit at stores and law enforcement officers. Windows were broken and merchandise was stolen, while your local city councilmembers are voting to cut down or eliminate police funding. Are all of your elected officials brain damaged?"

"Yes, they are," I said. "But no more so than elected officials throughout many of the states."

"This sounds like a great topic to discuss once we get to rural Arizona," Zack said. "There are a lot of bad things that happen today that wouldn't have been thought of back in the 1940s."

"A lot of things have changed for the better since then, as well," Sky said. "We now have vaccines to handle many deadly diseases, as well as a variety of medical breakthroughs unheard of during the first half of the 20th Century. Our country sent astronauts to the moon in 1969 and now civilian air travel is down to a matter of a few hours to go anywhere in the country. And, since the 1970s, the Ku Klux Klan doesn't rule the south anymore."

"Good!" Jones exclaimed. "I'm from Indiana. My grandfathers were Yankees. One of them was a hardcore abolitionist who helped found the Republican Party, primarily for the abolishment of slavery. And that led to Lincoln, who was the greatest president this country ever had."

"I just read that the Abraham Lincoln Elementary School in the Frisco area is being renamed," I said. "It seems the local politicos claim Lincoln didn't do enough for black people. In fact, they labeled him a racist."

"Now that's just outright insane!" Jones exclaimed.

"I haven't read anything about you ever being involved in politics," Zack said.

"I'm a film actor," Buck explained. "My job was to entertain, not pontificate. Our movies had positive-morality storylines. That's as political as I got. Like all good Americans, I voted. And I knew the KKK was an evil organization that had a lot of kinship with Germany's National Socialists. But powerful studio producers wanted their movies to be distributed in the south. They knew the Confederates, southern Democrats, would block any film critical of their party's savage Klansmen or their restrictive policies."

"Elected officials, who wanted to keep being elected, made sure it was 'politically incorrect' back then to say anything critical of the racist Klan," Lucky explained.

"Life had its craziness in those days, as well," Zack said. "I think we can have some pretty interesting conversations concerning current events, knowledge from Buck's experience and, I'm assuming, a plethora of memories recounted by Lucky."

"You betchum, Red Ryder," Lucky added, while crunching on a strip of bacon.

"I'd like everyone to pack enough clothing to last five days," Zack said. "We'll return on December 23."

"Good," I said. "I still have to get Sammy's presents to my sister's house."

"I've had suitcases placed in your rooms," Zack said.

"Don't worry about me," Lucky added. "I travel light."

Zack stood up. "I'm going to get a few things packed into our vehicle. Let's meet in front of the building in one hour."

"Wilco," I said. I looked at Sky. "Do you have a boyfriend or anyone you need to tell that you'll be out of town for a few days?"

She smiled at me, winked and left the room.

"Sky one, Dave zero," Buck announced.

I went back to my apartment and packed my toothbrush, razor and goodies, plus three pairs of Levis, five clean western shirts and enough underclothes to avoid embarrassing myself if I were to get run over by a truck. (My mother would have approved.)

It didn't seem like a whole hour when I met Sky in the reception room.

"Buck, Zack and the invisible man are out front waiting for us, Romeo," she said.

"I'm sorry if my question about a boyfriend embarrassed you."

"Not at all, Dave. Keep it up."

She smiled, picked up her suitcase and went out the front door, while I stood flatfooted and stared at her. Then I grinned and followed along.

"Wow!" I exclaimed, as I gazed on our pristine, classic, wood-sided transportation. "A 1940 Ford Deluxe Station Wagon!"

Zack stood facing me, holding the driver's side door open. "Yep. And it's mine. So I'll drive."

"She's a beauty," Buck said.

We tossed our luggage in the back. Buck climbed into the front passenger side, while Sky and I took the middle bench seat and Lucky stretched out in the third seat next to our luggage.

The big engine rumbled as we pulled away from Sundance Labs. Zack got us on the freeway and, since we were too late for the morning rush, it didn't take long to get through the Inland Empire and out to Interstate-15 headed toward Barstow. The conversation was light. I believe Lucky took a nap until we climbed Cajon Pass and drove into Victorville.

"Hey," Buck said. "We just passed by Roy Rogers Ranch Road."

"Yep," I said. "The singing cowboy and his wife, Dale Evans, lived on their ranch here and operated a popular museum for many years."

"It looks like his King of the Cowboys status has lived on."

"It has," I answered. "But if you think that's cool, wait 'till I take you to Disneyland. Perhaps we could also fly out of John Wayne Airport, or drop by the President Ronald Reagan Library."

"I guess I have a lot to learn."

We stopped to fill the tank and visit the restrooms at Barstow. Then I bought five diet Pepsis and a bag of cookies while Zack pumped the gas.

"It's hard to get used to seeing people pump their own gas," Buck said. "But I guess it makes sense in such a populated society."

"They don't give away dishes anymore either," Zack said. "I'm sure all those cuts helped the stations with their overhead expenses."

We got back on the freeway and, almost immediately, ramped onto Interstate-40 toward Needles.

"I always find this next two-plus-hours' drive to be a bit monotonous in that it really is miles and miles of nothing but miles and miles," Zack said.

"You should have driven it back when you had to use Route 66," Buck said. "If it weren't for all the little roadside stops along the way, most people would have never made it through this desert, especially in the summer."

"The abandoned remains of some of those roadside stops can still be found along a few areas of the old road that still exist," Zack said. "We're just lucky it's winter, since this chariot doesn't have air conditioning."

My mind wandered as we traveled on the long straight freeway. I was wondering what it had been like during the gold rush as the pioneers drove covered wagons through the area, when I felt a tap on my shoulder. I looked back and saw Lucky smiling at me. He pointed out my window at the sky. I looked up and, once again, felt like my reality had been yanked out from under my feet. Flying at about 2,000 feet above us was a large, green, winged dragon. And, as if it had sensed that I was watching, it quickly ascended up and into a cloud.

"I told you," Lucky smiled. "Now that you know they exist, you're one of the lucky ones who can see them."

"What's that?" Zack said over his shoulder.

"We'll explain later," I said. Then I turned back to Lucky and whispered, "You'll let me know if any banshees show up?"

"You can bet on it, pal."

Wonderful! I thought, while my head began to throb. Maybe I should have just stuck with writing freelance, low-budget puff pieces.

Then my blood pressure returned to normal quickly as I noticed the amazingly gorgeous Sky Blue had nodded off for a nap and, like at the theatre, her head was on my shoulder. Who cares about a dragon? I thought. Life was good.

We exited the freeway in Needles and immediately began searching for a place to get a cold drink, preferably beer. And we continued the search right up to when we crossed the bridge into Arizona.

"There we go!" Zack said. "The Malibu Bar and Grill."

The stucco-sided structure overlooked the Colorado River. It didn't look

...IT QUICKLY ASCENDED UP AND INTO A CLOUD.

like anything out of the ordinary, except that sandwiches and cold beer could be purchased inside. And that made it special. The gravel parking lot held a couple of pickup trucks, an Isuzu and three Harley Davidsons.

We entered the door, which sported a porthole window, apparently the only one in the building. The inside was dimly lit with lights hidden behind fake palm trees. Booths and tables were scattered along the back wall, while the bar was lined with metal stools. A woman with orange hair sat at one of the tables with a man wearing a suit and tie, as three leather-clad bikers laughed and talked while shooting pool on a coin-operated table.

The ancient bartender wore a stained Hawaiian shirt and a flipped-down sailor's cap, Gilligan-style.

"Five bottles of Miller Lite," I said. "And while you're at it, why is this place named the Malibu Bar and Grill?"

The old-timer didn't miss a beat, as he answered while gathering the bottles from behind the bar. "Because when California finally shakes enough to crumble into the ocean, this will be the west coast. And everyone wants to visit Malibu Beach."

"That works for me," I said, as I paid him and, with Buck's help, carried the bottles to our booth.

"So how far are we from the ranch?" Buck asked.

"Not far," Zack answered. "It's the only dude ranch in north-west Arizona. It's on the western side of the Hualapai Mountains in Devil's Gulch. You'll love it."

"What's it called?" Sky asked.

"Wailing Banshee Ranch."

Oh, crap! I thought. Now what?

Lucky sipped his beer and avoided eye contact with me.

"I see the establishment serves roast-beef sandwiches," Zack said. "Who's up for a late-lunch?"

Following a quick unanimous vote, the professor walked to the bar and ordered five "special" sandwiches and another round of Miller Lites. Buck joined him to help bring over the beers. That's when there was a loud slam as a black pool ball jumped off the table and hit the floor, rolling near the bar. Buck reached down and picked up the eight ball.

"Hey! Grandpa! Toss it here," ordered a seedy looking man in torn Levis, black tank top and leather vest, red bandana wrapped over his greasy brown hair and dust-covered biker boots.

Buck stiffened, reached back and pitched a fastball over the plate and into the man's stomach. "Sure thing, sonny boy!"

The biker doubled over and fell to the floor. His two friends didn't take kindly to the situation. They were dressed about the same as their gasping pal. One of them sported a shaved head with a spider tattooed on the top. The other was a white guy wearing dreadlocks, something that should be completely illegal, and had to be forty pounds heavier than either of his friends.

Lucky and I rushed to stand with Buck.

"Take the beers to the table, Zack," I said. "We'll handle these guys."

Spider-head stepped up to me and glowered. I lifted my fists, ready for action.

"Ooh," spider-head said. "Are you a boxer? Let's just see how fast you are."

My invisible buddy smacked the man in the face twice.

"You want to see me do it again?" I asked, not having moved.

"Huh?" he said, while shaking his spider-topped head.

Then Lucky popped him in the nose really hard, knocking the thug back a couple of feet while he stared at me with confusion in his eyes. I blew on my right knuckles as if to cool them.

The overweight biker growled and rushed Buck, who stepped aside and slammed the bottom of his boot into the side of the man's knee. Dreadlocks fell to the ground with a squeal, grasping at his twisted leg. Spider-head then roared and leaped at me. And, according to Sky, an empty beer bottle lifted into the air and smashed across the top of the spider tattoo, dropping baldy next to the crying tough guy with dirty dreadlocks.

The man who missed catching the fastball got to his knees and pulled a cellphone out of his vest pocket. Although he was standing alone next to the pool table, an invisible foot kicked the cell out of his hand and crushed it into the floorboards. Then, close to his ear, a deep threatening voice sounding a bit like Orson Welles told him, "If you don't want to get an up-close view of the bottom of the river, go help your little friends crawl out of here. And don't ever come back!"

The biker scrambled to his hands and knees and crab hopped over to his wounded buddies. Once spider-head came to, they grabbed dreadlocks by his arms and dragged him out of the building. I had no idea how dreadlocks would be able to handle his motorcycle, and I didn't care. I just hoped we'd never see them again.

"The sandwiches and the last round of Miller Lite are on the house, boys," the smiling bartender said. "Those three assholes have caused a lot of damage, run off a good number of regulars and refused to pay for their drinks ever since they started coming here last week. Thanks for doin' whatever it was you did."

"No problemo, compadre," I said. "Malibu's just too nice of a place for their kind."

We sat down to enjoy our late lunch and laugh about a variety of things.

"Man, you really are fast," Lucky said to me. "You should enter the ring."

"Yeah. I really didn't know I had it in me."

"You know," Buck said. "That was fun."

"It would be nice to go out for a meal just once without you guys getting into a fight," Sky said.

"When we get to the ranch, there'll be plenty of time to relax and enjoy yourselves," Zack said. "There'll be barbecues, entertainment and lots of outdoor activities, including riding."

"It'll be great to get back in the saddle," Buck said. "I'm lookin' forward to leavin' the modern freeway system, portable telephones, big-screen Technicolor television pictures and political insanity and get on the trail and ride off into the wild."

"I've already scheduled a horse-trip campout for our second night at the ranch," Zack said. "So let's drink up and hit the trail."

We waved at the happy bartender and returned to the classic Ford. We were certainly pleased to see that the motorcycles were no longer in the parking lot. I figured the bikers were probably getting patched up at the local hospital.

We traveled up the road a ways and then turned east on Boundary Cone Road, where we passed through an old mining town that was trying extremely hard to be a tourist destination. We had to drive very slowly along the bars, restaurants and T-shirt shops, in that wild burros meandered along the street looking for handouts. Once beyond the business area, we hit a dirt road that went under a freeway and farther eastward up into the Hualapai Mountains. Soon we were in a thick pine forest.

Normally I liked going to the mountains. But there was something about this forest that gave me a chill. It was like I shouldn't be surprised if I saw a squad of dwarfs marching off toward their diamond mine, or an evil ax-man chasing a princess. Note to self, I thought. Avoid Hammer films and Disney movies, not necessarily in that order.

"The ranch is only another short mile," Zack said. "We'll turn at this gate with the WB on it."

"Warner Brothers?" Buck asked.

"Wailing Banshee," Zack answered.

I glanced back at Lucky, who looked to me like he was pretending to be asleep.

Overgrown trees created what seemed like a green tunnel around the gravel driveway. There were lots of rabbits, squirrels and even a few deer peeking at us through the foliage. The drive opened into a clearing in front of a large western farmhouse, barn, and bunkhouse. There were also storage structures, a chicken pen and what looked like a shack that probably contained rabbit hutches, as well as a well house and water tower.

We parked next to a couple of other cars, a multi-seated commuter van and two pickups with wooden racks in the back. On the other side of the opening were picnic tables, benches, wooden outdoor furniture and fire pits. Behind the buildings, the trees had been cleared for at least twenty-five acres of pastureland, which contained a few horses, close to a dozen steers and two Holstein milk cows.

"Nice spread," Buck said, as we stepped out of the Ford Station Wagon.

The front door of the white shiplap home flew open and a young couple came out to greet us. Both of them were wearing western attire, including large ten-gallon Stetsons. The young man was well over six-feet tall, had thick red hair and a matching bandana around his neck. The young lady, also a redhead, could have been a *Vogue* cover girl, if that magazine had catered to western ranch owners instead of insipid apartment dwellers.

"Howdy, professor," the man said while waving his big white hat. "Welcome to Wailing Banshee Ranch."

"Hey, Chet," Zack hollered. "I'd like you to meet Sky Blue, Dave Custer and Charlie Roberts. This is Chet and Irene McCroy."

We all grinned, shook hands and offered pleasantries.

"You're a lot younger couple than I thought you'd be when we spoke on the phone," Zack said.

"Thanks, I think," said Irene as she chuckled. "But we are the real McCroys."

I made a Walter Brennan reference, Buck and Sky looked confused and Zack laughed while Lucky stood back and kept quiet.

"So, Chet," I said. "Why is your ranch named Wailing Banshee?"

The couple chuckled.

"We get that question a lot," Chet said. "There aren't any ghosts here. My grandparents were the original owners back in the 1940s and they just wanted an Irish theme to the place. And we've continued the family traditions. For instance, if you're still here for Christmas, we'll be havin' corned beef and cabbage."

"And, we have a lot of owls around here who some nights get their feathers ruffled," Irene added. "Together, they can make a loud screeching noise that sounds like a screaming woman. Nothing to worry about."

"Owls, huh," I said, while watching Lucky out of the corner of my eye.

"Mr. Roberts," Irene smiled. "You look familiar. Have you been here before?"

"No, ma'am," Buck said. "But I've sure been looking forward to our stay."

"Well come on in," she giggled. "We'll get all y'all squared away in your rooms and the bar is open."

As we entered the southwestern-style building, we were met by the welcome smell of bread baking in an oven. Just inside the front door was a Queen Anne table with four western caps on it.

"As per your instructions, Zack," Chet said. "These are your chapeaus. You can't be cowboys without cowboy hats."

Zack picked up a large, white, wide-brimmed, ten-gallon hat and handed it to Buck. "Here you go, Charlie," he said. "It's just like the one worn by your favorite movie cowboy."

Buck grinned, took off his baseball cap, put on the Stetson and transformed into the classic Rough Riders star.

"Holy high-heeled moccasins!" Irene gasped. "You look exactly like Buck Jones!"

"He does, doesn't he," Zack said. "Charlie has even made a few dollars just hangin' around Hollywood Boulevard with the Chaplin, Monroe and Brando lookalikes."

"Are you a western film fan?" Buck asked Irene.

"You bet! That's why Chet and I love this place. We get to live the cowboy lifestyle while earning a decent living. And, tonight out by the fire pits we're going to show 'Hang 'Em High,' a classic Clint Eastwood western."

"Who?" Buck asked.

"He's just kiddin'," I said. "Charlie loves all the great western films."

"As do I," Sky said. "Ain't that right, Dave?"

"Oh, yeah! One of my most enjoyable evenings was at a theatre recently watching a Hoot Gibson film with Sky." And it was.

Zack put on his Stetson, grinned and looked very much like a bearded scientist in a western hat, while I didn't look quite as heroic as I had hoped when I put on my big white Ken Maynard-style sombrero. I probably looked more like the low-budget stuntman from "Death Valley Rangers." But Sky's hat transformed her into a blonde version of Raquel Welch from "Hannie Caulder."

"We're a bit informal around here," Irene said. "So here are the keys to your rooms, which are down the hall to the left."

She handed each of us a key and pointed toward the hallway. I picked up Sky's suitcase in my left hand and mine in my right. Buck rolled his eyes as we went to our rooms. I dropped Sky's bag in front of her door and then went to mine. Our invisible Buddy Holly was right behind me.

"I never get my own room," Lucky said.

"Maybe you would if other people could see you."

"That ship has sailed," he responded. "Right now, you and Buck are the only ones lucky enough to see Lucky."

"I feel so special. Anyway, Buddy Holly doesn't really fit in at a dude ranch."

"You're right."

Light flashed in the room. When my eyes readjusted, I was looking at Steve McQueen as Josh Randall from the "Wanted: Dead or Alive" television program, including the sawed-off Winchester "mare's leg" the actor wore in the show.

"How's this?"

"A bit unnerving," I said. "But since that show came along in the late '50s I don't think Buck will have trouble getting used to you."

The southwestern-style room was large and contained a double bed, armoire, recliner, refrigerator, table and three chairs, as well as a private bathroom. Two prints of Frederic Remington paintings were framed on the walls on each side of the window, which was covered by tribal-design drapes. I tossed my bag in front of the armoire and checked the refrigerator. It contained a six-pack of Miller High Life. I grabbed two bottles, twisted the lids off and handed one to Josh Randall.

"Once again, you can have the recliner tonight. I'll take the bed."

As soon as he finished his beer, Lucky opened the door. "I'm gonna check the place out." Then, before leaving, he looked back at me and said, "See ya, now hear?"

What a ham, I thought. I also realized I had better alert Buck before he saw the armed Josh Randall amble down the hall and said something to him, not realizing that he's talkin' to good old invisible Lucky.

I picked up the phone by the bed and punched in Buck's room number. The big cowboy answered after the second ring.

"I'm just givin' you a heads-up about Lucky," I said.

"What has he done now?"

"He's no longer that nerdy guitar strummer," I explained. "He's a cowboy."

"Who's he pretendin' to be this time? Johnny Mack Brown?"

"Nope. Just look for a guy with a sawed-off Winchester strapped to his leg."

"I hope he doesn't sing."

We agreed to meet in the den in a half hour. I dialed Zack and then Sky, both of whom said they would meet us at that time. I went into the bathroom and threw cold water in my face. Looking at my reflection in the mirror, I thought about our situation. It was time that we all shared a little knowledge, like why Zack had really brought us to the ranch. I wanted to know more about exactly what Lucky was. If he were actually able to have visited historic events of the past, could those people have seen him? And what was the story with that dragon?

I freshened up and left my room. The hallway was empty, which brought another thought to my mind. Where were all the other guests?

Upon entering the southwestern-style den, Sky calmed my thoughts with her lovely smile. She had changed into a Roy Rogers-like western shirt, boots, Levis just tight enough to destroy my concentration, and her new Stetson. Zack was seated at a large heavy-wood table that held two pitchers of beer and five glasses. I sat down and poured Sky and me each a glass of the amber liquid as Buck entered the room.

"So where's Buddy Holly?" Sky asked.

"He's just lookin' around," I said. "And he isn't Buddy Holly anymore. He's Steve McQueen as Josh Randall."

"I think we need a program to keep up with all the cowboys and aliens and all their aliases," the lovely blonde cowgirl said. "So how are you Mr. Jones? Or should I say Mr. Roberts?"

"Anyone as pretty as you, Miss Blue, can call me anything you want," the big ham tipped his hat.

The large windows, like the one in my room, were framed by tribal-design drapes. Beautiful western paintings hung on all of the walls, surrounded by photographs of the ranch from prior years with many celebrity visitors, such as Dick Foran, Barry Goldwater, Robert Taylor, Barbara Stanwyck, Jack and Tim Holt, and a teenaged Shirley Temple. The only thing that seemed out of the western theme was a painting over the fireplace of a red-bearded leprechaun.

The door swung open and cowboy Lucky entered the room.

"Pull up a chair, bounty hunter," I said.

Lucky hopped into a recliner, leaned way back, crossed his boots on the footrest and tilted his hat forward over his eyes. Buck looked at him like he was an idiot. I turned to Jones and said, "He's a 1950s anti-hero."

"Seems more like a cocky jerk."

"Okay, Lucky," I said. "It's time to explain a few things. You say you were at some specific events in our history. Were people able to see you in those days?"

"Some could. Some couldn't."

"You alluded that you may have been at the Little Big Horn."

"I was. Most of the Indians were able to see me, except when I didn't want them to. I brought Custer into the visual loop."

"And how did that come about?"

"Your indigenous peoples had open minds," he said. "They believed in spirits and other things that weren't physical. Therefore, they could see me, dragons and a variety of forest spirits."

"And Custer?" Buck asked.

"Old Yellow Hair had a bit of a problem with night terrors," he explained. "What he didn't know was that night terrors are real creatures that prey on certain people who have receptive abilities, and feed on their fears. I appeared one evening when he was in his tent battling with his demonic visions. I stepped in and vanquished them, temporarily. And when the cavalry commander completely awakened, I was still there."

"And today, only Buck and I can see you, but everyone can hear you," I said. "Would you care to elucidate?"

"I told you," he stated. "The three of us were spiritually joined in the time dimension. As I stay in your world, I can allow people to see me. It's just that I like to check them out first."

The television cowboy stood up, walked over to the table and placed one hand on Zack's shoulder and one on Sky's. Light flashed in the room.

"And there you are!" Sky exclaimed.

"Damn!" Zack added.

"Your Steve McQueen-look is perfect," Sky said. "It's nice to finally meet you, Lucky."

"Back at ya, babe!" He pointed at her and snapped his fingers.

"Now, Lucky," I said. "What about dragons?"

"Dragons haven't been seen in this world for centuries," he explained. "Oh, they're there. It's just that they live peacefully because no one, up until now, has been able to see them."

"Do we have to worry about them?" Zack asked.

"Nope. They're a very private species from another dimension. And as long as they are invisible to your world, they can lead happy lives."

"Do they know that I've seen one of them?"

"They do. But as long as you don't threaten them, they won't harm you."

"What do they eat?" Buck asked.

"I understand they are partial to wolf, coyote and venison."

"And you mentioned banshees, tribal spirits and ghosts," I said.

"Those are not from other dimensions," he said. "They are of your world. But, they have been forgotten, especially in your industrialized nations. Your people don't believe in them anymore."

"But you're saying they're still there?"

"I am. And now the four of you are able to see them as well."

Great! I thought. I felt like we were unwary travelers at the beginning of a Peter Cushing film, who had decided to spend the night at Castle Dracula.

"Are we in danger?" Sky asked.

"You're mortal," Lucky said. "Of course you're in danger. But no more than you were yesterday or the day before."

"This has been very enlightening," Zack stated. "Which is one of the reasons I planned this vacation."

"You know, Zack," I said. "I haven't seen any other guests in this establishment."

He smiled. "For one, it's winter, off season. And the other reason is because I reserved the whole ranch for our use. I figured, without too many outside influences, it would be easier for Buck to segue into the new century while he could still enjoy his western roots."

"No other hidden agendas?" I asked.

"Well, there are a couple of things that I need to discuss with everyone," Zack answered. "But for right now, I'm just pleased to learn more about Lucky's experiences and knowledge of extraterrestrial and supernatural entities about which, up until today, I had been unaware."

"I checked out the bunkhouse," Lucky reported. "The ranch has a full staff to take care of the livestock, cook meals and prepare for festivities. So we're not quite alone."

"That's right," Sky added. "We're supposed to see a western film out by the fire pits tonight following supper. I hope those fires can keep us warm out there after dark."

I wiggled my eyebrows and smiled. "I wouldn't mind sharing one of those nice thick southwestern throw blankets, if you are so inclined."

Sky smiled.

Lucky changed the subject. "You and I need to talk a little about your time travel efforts," he said to Zack. "I realize a lot of planning went into your ability to go back in time without impacting the time continuum. But there are other things to worry about."

"Such as?"

"Such as hitchhikers, like me," Josh Randall explained. "You were lucky that it was only me that tagged along."

We stared at the other-dimensional television cowboy.

"The time dimension is a jump-off point for all kinds of things," Lucky continued. "Some of them are kind, benevolent, talented and good looking, like me. But some are malevolent entities that leave a trail of destruction."

"Can you be more specific?" I asked.

"There are creatures that are able to overpower the minds of mortals. They create horrible situations simply by manipulating stupid beings that may never even know of the evil creature's existence."

"Can they be seen?"

"Not by most people. Animals are aware of them, and do their best to avoid the creatures. Now, you four are anointed. You are now able to see a lot of things of which mankind has been unaware."

"That's a lot to think about," I said, as I stood up to stretch my legs, walked to the window and looked out at the livestock meandering around in the pasture. Standing near a few of the horses were a half dozen Native Americans wearing loincloths and not much else.

"Where'd all the Indians come from?"

"And there you have it," Lucky said as he joined me at the window. "Those are simply a few tribal spirits watching over the horses."

As if they heard us, all of the natives turned and looked toward our window. Then, they faded from view, only to reappear standing along the tree line and backing up into the brush to vanish once again.

"Tribal spirits protect nature as much as they can," Lucky lectured. "Those spirits are mostly benevolent. If you are willing to listen, they may even be a help to you in certain cases. It's the living you need to worry about, not the dead."

That old Hammer Film feeling washed over me again with an icy finger running up my spine.

The door opened and Irene McCroy walked in carrying a tray with a full pitcher of beer on it.

"We figured you might have need of a fresh one," she said, as she set the pitcher on the table. "Supper will be ready in an hour. If you need anything else, just holler." She then left the room and closed the door.

Sky picked up the pitcher and topped off our glasses. "Let me see if I can cut to the chase," she said. "We came out here to have a little R&R and, perhaps, decompress from our recent time travel experiment. But now, we are able to see Lucky as well as a variety of dragons, spirits and possibly evil demons. I hope this isn't going to be deducted from my earned vacation time."

CHAPTER SEVEN
FOREST FRIENDS

Our dinner was steak, baked potatoes, green beans and beer served on a picnic table near one of the fire pits. Most of us had apple pie for dessert, except for Buck who just fired up a Honduran cigar. A few bats staggered across the night sky while we laughed and shared stories from all of our pasts. Even though he would probably have told the best stories, Lucky wisely remained quiet.

Once we finished our meal, Irene removed our plates and silverware, including the extra ones that had been placed in the "empty" spot, while Chet wheeled out a film projector and transferred it to a heavy metal stand. We moved closer to the fire pit and got comfortable in some wooden patio furniture that faced a large white canvas sheet which had been stretched between two trees. Sky and I shared a comfortable wooden swing that hung from a big oak branch. And, of course, I had remembered the southwestern-style throw blanket.

The sky displayed its endless array of stars, which seemed to tell us how insignificant we really were, in a good way. I could hear a couple of owls hooting at each other in the distance. And the coyote communication grapevine seemed to be very busy deep in the woods. At least I hoped they were owls and coyotes, and not otherworldly things.

Chet flipped on the projector, the sheet became lighted, and we all leaned back to enjoy "Hang 'Em High." I had always been a fan of Eastwood's westerns. Like the classics of Randolph Scott and Gary Cooper made during the mid-to-late 1950s, they were well constructed with defined characters and amazing action sequences more tightly choreographed than a Busby Berkeley musical. Several times during the movie I looked over at Buck to see his reaction. Most of the time he seemed completely engrossed with the film.

At the movie's conclusion, Jones stood up, looked at me and said, "Wow!"

"Other than that, Mrs. Lincoln, how did you like the play?" Lucky asked.

"They've made some wonderful advancements in western filmmaking," Buck said.

"Yes. That's the good news," I said. "The bad news is, they haven't made very many westerns in the last thirty years, and no good ones at all during that time period."

"It would be hard to top that one," he said.

"Wait until you see 'Unforgiven.' In fact, as time goes on I'm going to expose you to 'The Searchers,' 'High Noon,' 'The Magnificent Seven,' 'Ride the High Country,' 'Seven Men From Now,' and a plethora of other masterpieces."

"We probably better go inside," Sky said.

"Oh, I don't know," I said. "I'm pretty warm and comfortable right here with you under this blanket."

"I think I'd be more comfortable in my warm bed."

"Now that you mention it, I think I would too."

That didn't go over as well as I hoped, as she yanked the blanket off of us and stomped back toward the ranch house.

"Sky two, Dave zero," Buck said, while grabbing his empty beer bottle and following the blonde beauty back into the building.

Zack, Lucky and I walked together.

"There's one other reason we are here that I need to tell you," Zack said. "You are probably aware that there is a big problem in this country concerning industrial espionage."

"I've read a few articles about technology thieves," I said. "Some of whom were being sent by foreign governments to steal research materials. But a whole heck of a lot of the theft is being done by computer hackers located in enemy countries."

"We've had some recent attempts to get into Sundance Laboratories," Zack said. "We have extreme security measures that prevent anyone from accessing our buildings or our computers. All of our projects are on freestanding computer systems, none of which have any links to the Internet or any other outside entities. But since our employees live away from our facility, we're a little worried that they have been surveilled. I'm talking about Sundance Laboratories and all of our subsidiary companies. Some employees' homes have been bugged. Their cellphones and home computers are compromised and I'm beginning to learn that their lives are in danger."

"How many people are we talkin' about?" I asked.

"Well, most of our team is right here," Zack said, "except for Beth. But we have chemical, pharmaceutical and electronics companies that service our facilities. I'm a bit worried about everyone connected with us.

"I've made arrangements for Beth to stay within our facility walls. The building is locked and the National Security Agency is watching it. I temporarily cancelled our janitorial service, which is a subsidiary company that I also own. I brought you, Buck and Sky out here where I think we are safe, for the time being. The NSA is currently all over the problem in Torrance, and I'm hopin' they will track down the culprits and nail them before we get back."

"Do you think it's the commies or radical Islamists?"

"Could be either," he said. "Or it may be just some unethical big R&D operation. Our skin tissue and organ research alone will be worth billions in the future. But if the wrong people get ahold of it, humanity would be the loser. And our time-travel successes definitely cannot be allowed in the hands of unscrupulous men who might try to exploit time manipulation for profit."

"You mean someone who wants to bet all the winners at the races?"

"That's about it," he said. "And such behavior could bring about big losses for the human race."

Once we got to our rooms, I brushed my teeth and prepared to go to bed. When I left the bathroom, I saw Lucky already curled up under his blanket on the recliner.

"When we get back, we need to double-check my place for listening devices," I said.

"I could probably be a help in finding out just who is bugging you folks," Lucky said. "We'll clear out any conversation-tapping devices from your home. Then I'll just hang out there for a couple of days. If someone comes in to re-plant listening devices, your favorite invisible friend will be on the spot to see who does it and to tag along with them to wherever it is they hang out."

"I think you've got somethin' there. Your transparency is really gonna come in handy. Let's discuss this with Zack in the morning."

I rolled over and sleep hit me like a Chuck Norris kick to the head. My dreams were filled with spooky Indians riding milk cows, dragons wearing fedoras, trench coats and old-fashioned earphones while listening to private conversations, and a yellow-haired cavalry officer on a white horse trying to order a happy meal in the McDonald's drive-through lane. Considering my recent reality, nothing seemed strange in dreamland at all.

•••

"You gonna sleep all day?" Lucky's voice invaded my brain.

"Blrgh."

"I understand breakfast is being served," he said. "And you need to open your eyes and get ready for an exciting day!"

"Bllap, flugha."

"My thoughts exactly. But still, Sky is probably already downstairs. And I think she might have a thing for one of the cowhands who's coordinating today's ride. She's probably already flirting with him out by the bunkhouse."

I jumped to my feet, frowned at the television bounty hunter and ran to the bathroom. I quickly showered, brushed my teeth and got dressed in clean western clothing. My mirror told me I looked pretty sharp, other than the few pieces of toilet paper on my face from having shaved a little too quickly. A short fifteen minutes later I sat down next to Sky at the breakfast table.

Lucky leaned in close and whispered, "I lied about the bunkhouse cowhand."

I snarled at the mean man and poured my first cup of coffee for the morning. And it didn't take too long to have a positive impact on my demeanor. I turned and smiled at Sky who cringed as a small piece of bloody toilet paper dropped off my face and into my coffee. I reached into the cup and removed the floater.

"I nicked myself while shaving," I explained.

"I noticed," she said. "You really aren't much of a morning person, are you?"

"Nope."

"We're gonna start the day with a little target practice," Zack announced while passing me a plate of bacon. I forked a couple of strips and then scooped a pile of scrambled eggs onto my plate.

After the morning meal we followed Zack out the parlor's French doors and into the open area behind the house where we found a picnic table covered with delightful weapons. There were three leather belts with holsters, which contained Colt .44 Magnum double-action revolvers. Another smaller, ladylike leather belt held a Smith and Wesson .38 five-shot revolver in a light-blue denim holster. Next to the revolvers were a Springfield M1903 bolt-action rifle and three AR-15s along with several loaded magazines and boxes of ammunition.

"I thought Buck might appreciate the Springfield," Zack said.

"I do," Jones replied. "Those other rifles look a little too Flash Gordonish for me."

"They're like any other semi-automatic," I said. "The anti-gun people all seem to freak out about the AR-15s, but they have the same abilities as practically any other deer rifle."

"I'm still comfortable with the bolt-action M1903," Buck said. "That rifle and I share a bit of history."

"Now these Colt .44s are modern double-action six-guns with a lot of power," Zack said.

"Yeah, just ask Clint Eastwood," Sky added.

"Who?" Buck questioned.

Lucky leaned in close and whispered, "Hang 'Em High."

"Oh," Buck said. "That guy."

A variety of targets were placed in the field in front of us, starting at about fifty feet away and continuing haphazardly up to two hundred feet. The closest were about the size and shape of the front area of a prone enemy. The farthest targets were man-size standing shapes.

"Although this is a fun and safe recreational activity," Zack said, "I've set these cardboard targets up to represent enemy terrorists, soldiers or just plain old bad guys."

I strapped on one of the .44s while Sky belted her Smith and Wesson around her shapely denim-covered hips. Buck and Zack followed suit, while Lucky grabbed an AR-15, slammed a banana clip in it and hollered, "Let's kick some cardboard ass!" He flipped the selector switch from safe to fire and started blasting away at one of the farthest targets, ripping a heart-sized hole in the center of its chest area.

"Damn, spook!" Buck exclaimed. "You're one hell of a shot."

Sky drew her revolver and popped a hollow-point slug through the head area of one of the prone targets. Buck smiled, took a piece of gum out of his pocket, started chewing it and, with lightning speed, drew his Magnum and ripped the head off another prone target. "Buck Roberts nails another one," he said, alluding to his on-screen character.

"That's *Charlie* Roberts, Buck," Zack said.

"Hey, Lucky," I said. "Show us what you can do with that mare's leg."

Josh Randall gripped his cut-down Winchester carbine, squinted his eyes

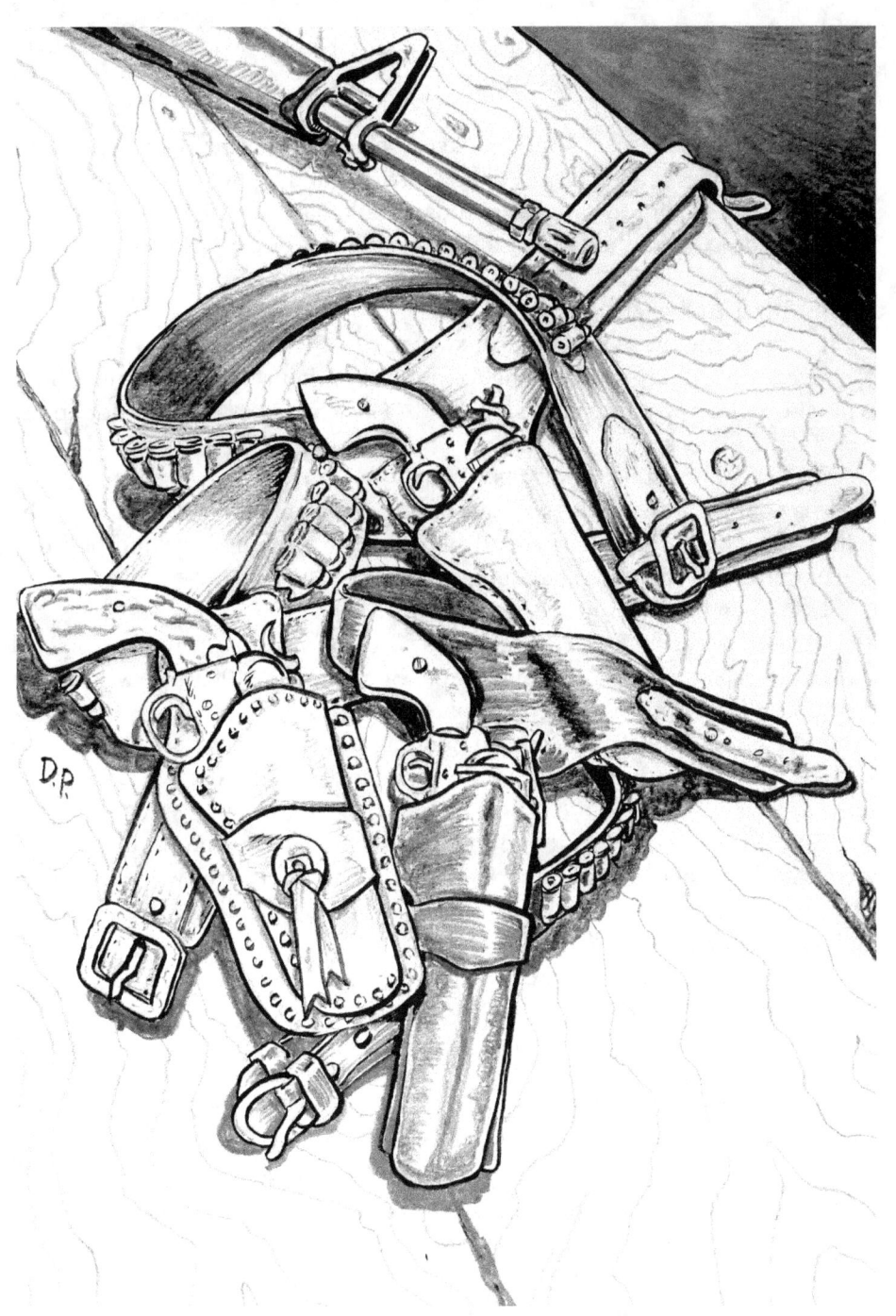

THERE WERE THREE LEATHER BELTS WITH HOLSTERS...

and fired from the hip. A lot of gun smoke accompanied the loud blasting from the weapon, but no target was hit.

"You missed," Sky stated.

"Yep," Lucky explained. "But it looked cool, didn't it? This is just part of my costume. It's like a movie prop. All noise, smoke and no bullets."

"When we ride out toward camp today, you'll have an AR-15 in a scabbard on your saddle," Zack told Lucky. "We'll all have our weapons with us, just in case."

"Just in case of what?" I asked.

"Just in case we need them," he answered.

We continued target practicing for close to an hour before Zack told us to wind it up. "Keep your revolvers," he said. "Grab plenty of ammunition to put in your jacket pockets."

"My jacket doesn't have pockets," I said.

"I have new leather jackets for all of us," Zack announced. "Irene will be joining us on our ride. Our bedrolls will contain sleeping bags and pup-tent shelter-halves, as it is very cold up here at nights."

"It's cold up here during the day," I added.

"Attached to each AR-15 rifle scabbard will be a bag containing three loaded banana clips," the professor continued. "Buck. Your M1903 bag will have a half-dozen five-round stripper clips plus extra rounds."

"Every saddle will have a canteen hanging from the horn," said Irene, who had just walked up. "I'll bring some canned beans and fruit, bread and beef jerky as well."

"Next to your jackets you'll find bayonets that can attach to your pistol belts," Zack said. "One of the most important things to bring into the woods is a good knife. I'm sure you can think of a dozen uses for it, including digging a small cat hole when needed."

"What's a cat hole?" Sky asked.

"Either one of you vets want to enlighten her?" the professor asked.

I leaned in close and did the honors.

"Oh," Sky said.

Then she started to ask a question but was cut off by Irene. "Small military toilet paper rolls are in the saddlebags, along with mess kits, matches, first-aid supplies, two extra pairs of boot socks and other necessities.

"We also have crossbows and arrows in the barn, if you want to try them on the targets before we wrap up here," she added. "A lot of our guests enjoy them more than traditional archery."

"Not this time," I said. "Maybe later."

We returned to the ranch house to gather our jackets, bayonets and underwear, as well as to have our final visits to the indoor plumbing. Zack told us to leave our cellphones in our rooms, as reception was sketchy on the mountain anyway. Irene went to the barn to assist staff in saddling our horses and tying on our bedrolls, ropes and equipment.

I went to my room and washed up. While there, I removed the small compass from my overnight bag and stuffed it in my pocket where I would usually have kept my cell, took my toothbrush, a small tube of toothpaste and my roll-on deodorant to place in my saddlebag and switched my undershirt with a sweatshirt that sported a picture of Grumpy from Disney's "Snow White" (a gift from my sister).

Once back in the living room, I tried on my new brown leather jacket, which, like all the others, had a logo and the word Sundance on the back. I figured the R&D scientist wrote them off his taxes as promotional advertising. The bayonet sheath easily attached to my new pistol belt. Shoving my Stetson squarely on my head, I confronted Zack.

"So we're gonna ride off into the woods and spend the night on the side of a mountain in the dead of winter," I said to the scientist.

"Didn't you always want to grow up and be a cowboy?" he asked.

"Well, yeah."

"This is what cowboys did; spring, summer, fall and winter. And I think it will be good for Buck's mental state."

"But do you think it's safe for Sky to be out there away from all civilization?"

"The farther we get from civilization, the safer we are. You know there are people trying to track us down right now. If we can stay off the radar long enough for the feds to nail the monkeys who are after us, we'll be home free."

"Well, I guess you're right, professor. And you've certainly taken us to the most off-the-radar spot in the country."

Irene entered the building and walked up to us. "We've got six horses saddled and ready for our ride," she said. "And I know you were adamant. But why six *saddled* horses with five riders?"

Zack grinned. "There's a very interesting answer to that, Irene. But, for now, I just suggest you observe as we ride. That way, when we arrive at our campsite, it will be easier for you to understand our explanation."

All of the horses were calm, healthy Morgans. I chose a dark-brown, friendly looking gelding with a reddish mane and tail. He gave me a welcoming grin. Either that or he thought my big white hat made me look really stupid.

The leather rifle scabbards were unique in that they were open in an area to allow banana clips to stay loaded in the AR-15s. Belts wrapped around the weapons' buttstocks to make sure they were secure for the ride.

Buck mounted up first, followed by Zack and then Irene. I helped Sky into her saddle and then climbed on my friendly steed. The sixth horse stood next to Irene and her mount, as she held its reins.

"Just leave the reins free," Zack said. "The horse will follow us."

Irene looked at him strangely and then wrapped the ends of the reins around the saddle horn. I was sure that she was probably thinking, "The customer is always right. But in this case, the customer is nuts."

"Buck," Zack said. "Lead the way. Let's have a good ride and then find a site to set up camp."

Jones nodded, grinned and rode into the thick pine forest. Zack was next, followed by our "empty" horse, then Irene and Sky, with me riding drag. I could see Lucky holding his reins close to the horse's mane as he kept it moving along nicely in the crisp mountain air, much to Irene's bewilderment. All of us were wearing Sundance brown leather jackets, except for Lucky, which made us look like a cowboy version of the Flying Tigers. Of course, Josh Randall was too cool to have to wear a jacket.

Although the pine-scented air was chilly, it was fresh, clean and welcome to our Los Angeles smog-tainted lungs. Bushy tailed squirrels bounced through the trees around us as if they were happy spectators and we were their Hollywood Christmas Parade. And, like the good old days of that particular city event, the Grand Marshal was a legendary movie cowboy.

We reached an area where there was a little more room on the trail, which allowed me to ride up next to Sky, whose cheeks were delightfully pink from the crisp, cool air.

"Are we havin' fun yet?" I asked.

"I think so," the blonde beauty replied. "It's been years since I've ridden. And this wild woods area, as well as the diverse company, makes it quite special."

"Yeah. Out here away from everything is a bit like going back in time, again."

"This is today, Dave. Enjoy it."

I smiled at the gorgeous cowgirl and wondered what I could say that wouldn't come off like small talk. Then I realized any kind of friendly conversation with that lovely lady, even small talk, would seem delightfully important to me. Therefore, I decided to learn a little more about her.

"So how did you get hooked up with Sundance?" I said, knowing it was just slightly better of a question than "What sign are you?" or "Do you come here often?" Neither of which were applicable in the woodsy setting.

"Several years ago, I interned at the lab during my college senior year," she explained. "When I graduated, I just stayed on as a fulltime assistant while earning my master's degree. I was fascinated by the medical research successes coming out of the facility. The professor has such a creative mind that he foresees medical advances that others could never comprehend."

"The things I've seen are well beyond my imagination," I said.

"And that's just the tip of the iceberg. We have ongoing development of many lifesaving technologies that will revolutionize medical science for years to come."

She was obviously excited about the facility's scientific advancements, of which she had been a big part. Sky's career was definitely very important to her. I could understand that. We all need to find something to believe in, I thought. And I hoped that I would soon feel more comfortable in my role as a member of the Sundance team.

A doe and her fawn stood watching us at about twenty feet from our path. I looked into mother deer's eyes and saw no fear, like she knew we were not dangerous to her or her family. Then, only for about a second, I saw a loincloth-wearing Indian standing next to her. He vanished quickly.

"Did you see that?"

"Yes," Sky answered. "The deer were beautiful."

"I mean…"

"I also saw the tribal spirit," she said. "Lucky said they were not to be feared."

Yes, I thought. Lucky did say that. But then again, Lucky was somewhat of an otherworldly creature as well. I kept my eyes open and my head swiveling as I watched the forest for surprise visitors during our "pleasant" ride. I just hoped supernatural Indians didn't shoot real arrows.

"Let's take a break and give the horses a drink," Buck said, as he dismounted next to a crystal clear creek. "This clean water is comin' right off the top of the mountain."

A series of twenty-to-thirty-foot waterfalls rose up in front of us for a few hundred feet. Each level of majestic granite boulders broke up the stream and then reunited it again for another drop across naturally beautiful rocks. The pool at the base was ice-green and clear.

"If you need to fill your canteens, do so," Buck said. "Restrooms are over there." He pointed at several tall pine trees.

"Really?" Sky asked.

"No," I said. "He means cat holes, if needed, can be dug behind those tree trunks."

"Oh." She looked disappointed.

We led our horses to the water's edge. Irene watched as the rider-less mount walked forward to quench its thirst.

I traipsed quite a little distance to find the perfect tree for me to step behind and dampen a couple of forest plants. Once I had completed my chore, I zipped up my fly, turned around and found myself face to face with an ancient tribal warrior. His weathered face seemed fierce, as his eyes opened wide and bored into my soul. His left hand clutched my right shoulder, while my feet were frozen to the ground and my first thought was how glad I was that I had already peed.

Oh, God! I thought. I hope he doesn't know my last name!

Then he smiled. Sweeping his right arm out, he directed my gaze into the forest. Standing behind him close to a tall pine were the doe and fawn I had seen earlier. Both of them lightly stepped forward as the warrior reached down and scratched their ears. Then the fawn nuzzled my left hand. The fear washed from my body.

The deer turned and walked back into the forest. The warrior held up one finger, nodded at me and then motioned for me to look toward an area in the trees. Some leaves rustled and were pushed aside. At that moment, I realized I might have been a bit hasty in thinking I had nothing to fear. An approximately thirty-foot-long, olive drab, scaly dragon walked on muscular rear legs and sharp talons, helped along by its huge winged arms, toward me. Its head was the size of one of Spielberg's tyrannosaurus movie monsters. It blinked and then translucent film lids opened showing me bright yellow eyes that seemed to look through me.

My warrior friend stroked the beast's forehead, and it began to purr. He took my hand and placed it on the dragon's nose. Nervously I grinned and attempted to pet the creature between its nostrils. It snorted, backed up a step and shot out a long pink tongue that licked my face and then returned to its fang-filled mouth. The Indian nodded to the beast, which launched itself into the air and roared off like an Air Force F-22 Raptor.

The warrior then smiled and vanished. I stood there for a full minute, thinking about what had just happened. By the time I could move my feet and start walking back to my companions, I realized the tribal spirit just told me that we had nothing to fear. We were among friends, as unique as they were.

I was walking toward the creek when I heard the scream and broke into a run, as I recognized Sky's terrified voice. Holy crap! I thought. Is everybody getting introduced to monsters today? Buck and Zack had their guns in their hands while they rushed around trying to figure out Sky's location. I was the first to see her.

The wide-eyed beauty was crouched behind a tree with the bayonet in her hand. I ran up to her and saw she was thrusting the knife into the base of the pine tree over and over.

"It's a giant poisonous lizard!" she screamed.

I surveyed the scene. There was nothing around the base of the tree, other than the beautiful blonde scientist, who was squatting, yelling and stabbing. I also noticed her pants were down. I turned to face the other way, as I said,

"There's nothing there now."

"It was right here!" she yelled. "It hissed at me."

I looked over at a dried broken branch lying on the ground about ten feet away. Standing on top of it, a dark brown chuckwalla watched the research assistant's behavior from a safe distance.

"It's right over there," I said, pointing at the reptile. "He's just a friendly, non-poisonous chuckwalla. You don't have to be afraid of him."

"Why did he hiss at me?"

"Did you pee on him?"

The pretty blonde cowgirl, instantly realizing the position she was in, yelled for me to, "Get away!"

"Everything's okay," I hollered to the others.

I walked to the creek, topped off my canteen and hung it back over the saddle horn. I could have sworn my horse winked at me.

"I'm sorry, I…" Sky said upon her return.

"Not to worry," I replied. "Those things look scary."

"You'd be just as frightened as I was if you went to relieve yourself and was confronted by one of those ugly reptiles," she said.

"You are so right!"

CHAPTER EIGHT
JUSTICE FROM ABOVE

It didn't take Sky long to wind down. She even made a couple of awkward jokes about the situation. We all made sure to let her know that it could have happened to any of us. Then I motioned to Buck and Lucky to join me for a minute. Once we were out of earshot, I reported on my encounters.

"And the dragon was actually friendly," I said.

"Told you so!" Lucky exclaimed.

"I've seen a few of the tribal spirits along the trail," Buck said. "I think they're watching over us."

"Do you think they have a reason to watch over us?" I asked Lucky.

"Perhaps," our resident wraith said. "I just know, we're better off with them out there than without them."

We mounted up and rode close to three more hours before Buck held his hand up and stopped. We had arrived at a small clearing in the trees next to a little stream. The area looked like it would make a good campsite. Then the real work began.

Irene and Buck strung two picket-line ropes between trees next to the creek. We all removed the saddles and blankets from our horses while Buck spaced them out so they had the room to get at some of the grass beneath their hooves. Since we had six horses, the first fifteen-foot line would handle three and the second line between two other trees would secure the rest.

Then we had to set up the pup tents. Each of us carried a shelter-half with poles and pegs in our bedroll. Sky and Irene buttoned their halves together, while Buck and Zack built their pup tent. That left Lucky and me to be tent buddies. As the invisible troubadour and I struggled with our canvases, pegs and poles, I decided it might be a good time to explain things to Irene. Of course, I suggested Zack do the honors.

"That's the most ridiculous campfire story I've ever heard!" Irene said, following Zack's explanation.

"So how do you explain the horse's behavior on the ride?" the professor asked the dude ranch owner.

"My horses are used to trail rides," she stammered. "He just followed along like any well-trained animal would."

"Lucky. Strum your guitar."

The sound of an acoustic guitar drifted from our pup tent.

"That's a trick!" Irene spouted. "You've got a radio in there."

"Who's your favorite country music singer?" Zack asked her.

Irene thought for several seconds before she answered, "Red Foley!"

The deep melodious voice of Red Foley immediately launched into "Peace in the Valley," as Irene's jaw dropped.

"I meant to say, Hank Williams!" she hollered.

"Your Cheatin' Heart" rang out over the campsite. Irene dropped to sit on a fallen log.

"I give," she gasped. "You brought a ghost on the ride."

"Anybody want to hear 'Jambalaya'?"

"Not right now, Lucky," Zack said. "Irene. I just didn't want you to start doubting your own sanity from some of the things you might see. Lucky's not a bad guy. He's just different. And, he comes in handy when we're dealing with real bad guys."

"Whatever," the frustrated but resigned dude ranch owner said.

"Good-bye Joe, you gotta go, me oh my oh," Lucky sang.

"Later, Lucky!" Zack said. "Let's finish setting up camp."

All three pup tents were lined up on level ground. Once the pegs were pounded in and the tents tight, Buck and I used our bayonets to dig a slight trough around the sides for runoff in case of rain, while tossing the dirt onto the bottoms of the canvas to keep the cold air outside. The two of us then rolled a few short logs down to the tent area to be used as stools.

We then cleared an area for the campfire, while making sure no dry grass or flammable items were close to the fire site. About the time the sun was dropping out of view, we started the fire with kindling and strategically placed dry wood. A no-longer-sulking Irene McCroy dumped some canned beans in a pot and placed it in the fire.

"It's not a real cowboy camp without beans," she said.

I thought about that for a moment, looked over at Lucky and shook my head.

"Don't worry," he said. "If I feel the urge, I'll visit the squirrels."

"What did those squirrels ever do to you?" I asked.

Darkness dropped on us like one of Wile E. Coyote's anvils. We all leaned in to the fire to ward off the cold night chill. Irene slopped beans into our mess kits, which we enjoyed along with cold water and beef jerky. The topics of conversation were light, considering our earlier experiences. Lucky serenaded us with a selection of cowboy songs, singing with the voices of the cowboys who had originally sung them. Once again, I was amazed that that sentence made sense to me.

The night came alive with the sounds of the critters that lived there. They may not, however, have enjoyed the country western music as much as we did. Anyway, the coyotes were attempting to drown us out with their own choir. And then the screeching in the trees increased.

"Sounds like your owls are getting their feathers ruffled," I said to Irene.

The alleged hooting sounded a bit more like screaming to me.

"Yesterday I wouldn't have doubted it," she said. "But now, I don't know what to think."

The screaming got louder, sounding like a maniacal woman about to set someone on fire. Then we all stood up as a white cloud of mist swirled over us, slowly forming into a horrifying, shroud wearing, grizzled old crone with sharp teeth, long fingers and empty white eyes. Her screams caused us to cover our ears and back away. Buck fired his pistol dead center into the beast with no effect.

Lucky ran out in front of the fire and held his hands up. "Hold your fire! Keep calm!"

"Is that your ghost telling us to keep calm?" Irene yelled.

"Good question," I said. "Lucky! Is that thing going to do anything to us?"

The mist and the banshee woman vanished as quickly as she appeared.

"No!" Lucky yelled. Then he quietly said, "Like in the legends, banshees warn the living of danger."

"If that thing is just a warning," Buck said, "we're in for some bad shit!"

That's when we heard the whapping sound.

"Douse that fire!" I yelled. "That's a helicopter!"

We poured canteens of water onto the flames, then tossed beans and kicked dirt onto the ashes.

"Grab your rifles and ammo!" I said. "Let's move into those rocks above camp."

Someone had found us. I didn't know how or why, but I knew it was not a good thing. We scurried up through some thick brush into an area of large boulders; all the while my eyes darted around watching for snakes. I found a spot with good cover all the way around and placed Irene and Sky there.

"Just keep low and whomever is after us won't target you," I said. "Buck. Take your M1903 up about fifty feet to that high rock where you can hopefully see everything."

"It looks like a good sniper perch," the smiling cowboy said, as he scrambled up the rocks like a kid.

"Zack. Your field of fire will be from that V-shape in the boulders around twenty-five feet over there. I'll set up about the same distance in the other direction."

"I'm goin' down below," Lucky said. "Only you guys can see me, so don't shoot me."

"I don't know," I said. "It's getting a little dark."

Lucky began to glow a little. "How's this?"

"Great. Just leave your AR-15 with me," I said. "It won't help if they see a floating assault rifle."

I didn't know what was coming for us, but they had to have had some high-tech tracking equipment to be able to find us. Even Chet McCroy back at the ranch had no idea where we were. And we had left our phones in our rooms. Someone, I thought, must have planted a tracking device on one of us, probably while we were still in Los Angeles. I had a quick thought and yanked off my white Stetson, searched inside the liner and the band. There was nothing there. With modern technology, I thought, a tiny tracking device could have been hidden just about anywhere.

I could see Lucky in his Steve McQueen outfit skulking around the camp down below our positions. He looked up at me and pointed both to the right and the left. Then he crossed his arms and waited as several OD-green-fatigue-wearing thugs with Uzis closed in on our tents from both sides. They wore night-vision goggles and their weapons sported red laser sights. The men were wearing body armor and had grenades hanging from their web gear. I counted eight "soldiers" who didn't look like novices.

My mouth went dry as I realized we were definitely out-gunned. Holy shit!

I thought. We could put up a pretty good fight, but those Uzis and grenades could probably finish us off fairly quickly.

I just about jumped out of my skin, as Lucky appeared right next to me.

"You're gonna have to hold them off for a few minutes," he said. "I'm goin' for help."

Then he vanished. And almost instantly rock chips rained down on my head as one of the enemy gunners shredded a line of 9mm rounds across the granite above me. I jacked a 5.56mm round in the chamber of my AR-15 and leaned to the side of my barrier rock. I aimed at the offending asshole and fired two slugs into the dead center of his chest. He fell as his pals dived for cover and began firing in my general direction. Then I saw the soldier get back up. I had wasted two rounds on his body armor. He took aim at me once more, only to have the top of his head explode as a .30-06 round from our friendly neighborhood bolt-action sniper entered his forehead.

First blood put everyone on the edge. The enemy soldiers spread out along the bottom of the rocks and began their assault. They hammered my position while still trying to find other targets. Zack took one of them out with a bullet through the leg. He didn't kill him, but he put him out of commission, while one of the other troopers dragged the wounded man behind cover.

A few of the troops began to climb toward our positions. Every time I leaned out to get a shot at them, a barrage of enemy fire pushed me back. Zack was in the same fix. I knew that if the enemy were to be able to get much closer, they could finish us off with their grenades. And yet, I had to ask myself, why aren't they trying to capture us alive? If they were after the professor's research, they'd need the professor alive to make it work.

I could see one green-clad mercenary pull the pin on a frag grenade and reach back to throw it. Then his head exploded. The grenade dropped and his friends below him panicked as it bounced down toward them and exploded, sending shrapnel in all directions. Buck was doing well. I used the confusion to lean out across my rock protection and start randomly firing into the remaining troops.

Irene screamed and a shot was fired from the ladies' hideout. I scrambled like a chuckwalla across the rocks to reach them, only to find one dead soldier and no cowgirls. Sky's Smith and Wesson pistol was lying on the ground with a trickle of smoke coming up from the barrel. I shoved it in my left jacket pocket.

Several 9mm rounds hit the gravel around my boots. I dived for cover, rolled over on my shoulder and found my way back to my feet. A grenade exploded near Zack's position, sending rocks and dust into the air. Time was running out, I thought. At least one of these assholes has already captured Sky and Irene.

Zack could be dead or wounded and we were being blasted from three directions below. I take back what I said. Time wasn't running out. It had run out.

Then I heard an incredibly loud group roar and flapping as I looked up and saw three big green dragons dropping out of the sky. The enemy soldiers were confused, in that they could hear the beasts but couldn't see them. Talons and claws reached into the rocks and dragged one soldier up into the sky where my good pal, the dragon, shoved him into his mouth and chomped his razor-sharp teeth shut, ripping the man in half. His two friends screamed as they saw their comrade's legs drop to the ground next to them.

They didn't know where to shoot. It wouldn't have helped them anyway, as each of them were grabbed by one of the other dragons and lifted into the sky before they were eaten whole. Nothing was wasted.

I ran to Zack's position and saw that he was slightly wounded by some rock chips, but doing okay. I yelled, "Buck!"

"I'm fine!" he responded, while stepping out on the edge of a high rock. "One of the troopers has Sky and Irene! They're headed for the helicopter!" He pointed and I ran in the designated direction.

While gripping my AR-15 tightly, I moved as fast as I could on the uncertain terrain, in the dark. I knew which way the cowboy star had pointed and I did my best to keep going thataway. The path opened up and I could see a black tunnel in the shrubbery, which beckoned me forward. My feet flew out from under me and I dropped onto my butt to avoid running into the loincloth-wearing warrior who appeared in front of me. He reached down and helped me up, then pointed into the black tunnel, which was really an opening at the top of a cliff. Had I kept going, I would have found out what it was like to fly, for a couple of hundred feet straight down.

He motioned for me to follow and then started running parallel to the cliff. I stayed right on his heels. We arrived at an approximately three-hundred-foot-diameter clearing in the foliage with a helicopter sitting in the middle. I could see the enemy soldier herding Irene and Sky toward the chopper and I took off after them. My warrior friend slammed his shoulder into my side, knocking me to the ground just as a gaggle of 7.62mm rounds fired from a mounted M60 machinegun within the chopper tore up the area I had been running through.

I heard Sky scream as she had thought I had been taken out of the game. The soldier used his rifle butt to get her moving toward the helicopter. Irene had fallen and I realize the worst was about to happen. The soldier aimed his Uzi at the dude-ranch owner and smiled. Unfortunately for him, he didn't see or hear the scale-covered nightmare that swooped out of the sky and punctured his shoulders with powerful talons. The soldier squealed like a six-foot rat and dropped his weapon as he was lifted into the sky and ripped to shreds.

The chopper pilot decided it was time to leave. The engine roared to life and the propellers quickly increased their speed until the aluminum chariot floated upward. It was really too bad he couldn't see the dragon, which had flown over to face directly at where he sat in the cockpit. The big green legendary creature opened its mouth wide and seemed to take a deep breath before exhaling a massive Napalm-strike-size amount of flame that covered the tumbling, burning, melting, propeller-topped coffin.

Sky and Irene ran toward me with tears in their eyes. I met them halfway, and enjoyed the hugs immensely, especially those from my favorite blonde-haired beautiful scientist. I turned and my warrior friend was gone. But Buck had caught up with me and the four of us chattered away as we walked back toward our campsite. Sky's arm was still wrapped around my shoulders when Buck looked at me and winked. "And Dave hits it over the center-field wall."

"That works for me," she said.

We arrived back at the campsite to see Zack stacking Uzis over near the horses.

"We'll have to take these back with us," he said. "Lucky's AR-15 is also back in his scabbard."

"Where are all the enemy bodies?" I asked.

"A couple of dragons did an excellent cleanup for us," Zack said. "Have you seen Lucky?"

"I'm sure he'll be along in while," I answered. "He went to fetch help."

"And a fine job he did," Buck added.

I looked over toward the tents and saw that our campfire had been re-ignited and was burning very well.

"Let's go warm up," I said, just as I heard a guitar strum the beginning of "Blue Yodel No. 1."

"T for Texas, T for Tennessee. T is for Thelma, that gal made a wreck out of me."

Hearing Jimmie Rodgers amazing voice didn't bother us one bit. Even Irene thought it was nice. Of course she couldn't see the yodeling, guitar-strumming dragon leaning up against a tree by the campfire.

"Hey, guys," the dragon said.

"Back at ya, Lucky," Buck said. "Thanks for bringin' help."

"They're my cousins."

"We've got a couple of cans of peaches and some beef jerky," I added. "But I'll bet you're not interested in joining us for a snack."

"Not tonight," the Lucky dragon said. "I'm stuffed."

CHAPTER NINE
RANCH HOUSE ROUNDUP

We sat around the campfire for a little bit, trading thoughts about the recent action. Sky and I shared a log while we laughed and sang along with our guitar-strumming friend, who had changed his act to look and sound like Bing Crosby from Rhythm on the Range.

"I have to say that you do Bing very well," Buck said.

"My, my, my," the musical ham said. "Bartender. I'll have big, bubbly, bottle of Budweiser brew, boy," he added, with emphasis on the Bs.

"And with that, I think it's time for me to hit the sack," Sky announced.

I wiggled my eyebrows, and she added, "Irene. Are you as tired as me?"

The ranch owner nodded and she and Sky went to their pup tent and buttoned the entry flap behind them.

"I'm a bit tuckered out myself," Buck said. "How about you, Zack."

The scientist and the cowboy excused themselves and retired to their sleeping bags. Der Bingle and I were left to ponder our situation by the campfire.

"I don't think we'll have any other visitors tonight," I said. "But I'll keep watch for the first four hours if you'll spell me at midnight."

"Let me take the first watch," Lucky said. "I think you need the sleep. I'll wake you at twelve."

"Thanks. In the morning, we'll ride back to the ranch. Then we better skedaddle before our enemies send in another team."

I climbed into my sleeping bag in the warm pup tent and fell asleep faster than an attorney could show up following a traffic accident. I dreamed that I was serenaded by scarf and knit-cap wearing dragons singing Christmas carols, I jumped out of a biplane crop duster with sky-diving horses carrying Uzis and I watched and participated in a black and white movie with Buck Jones and Bing Crosby called "The Road to Ridiculous"—in other words, nothing out of the ordinary.

I awoke to the sound of an owl hooting in the night. My watch told me it was almost midnight. When I exited the pup tent, I saw Josh Randall and my tribal warrior friend seated on a log by the campfire laughing and talking in some strange language.

"Howdy, gentlemen," I said as I walked up behind them. "Both of you guys did very well out there tonight. And we appreciate it."

"Is it that time already?" Lucky asked.

"Yep. I'll take it from here."

The warrior stood up and smiled, then walked over toward the trees where he was met by the doe and fawn from earlier. They meandered off into the forest and vanished.

"It pays to have friends," Lucky said.

"It certainly does. Now, you better get some sleep. After all that flying, your wings are probably pretty tired."

I was left alone with the elements, which was just fine. The peace and quiet of the forest night was exactly what I needed. I tossed a couple of branches onto the fire and sat down on a log to keep watch. Lots of strange things clattered around in my mind, but the most important were my questions about what would come next. For one, we had to get back to the lab safely. And we needed to figure out how we were tracked and who was doing the tracking. With a little luck, perhaps Zack's federal friends would have a few answers for us upon our return.

Following about two hours of frenetic thinking, I walked over to where the horses were picketed. They all seemed fine. They could reach water and there was plenty of grass around their hooves. My horse, that I had decided to call Bob, was awake and grinning at me. I stroked his mane and scratched his ears.

"Well, Bob. It looks like you're headin' home in the morning. So if you've got a little mare-friend back in the barn, you'll see her tomorrow." I paused. "I don't know. Do geldings have mare-friends?"

When I turned to walk back to the fire, Bob tried to bite me on the butt. I looked at him and thought, okay. I shouldn't have made the "gelding" remark.

I reached into one of my saddlebags and found my toothbrush and a small metal cup containing packets of instant coffee. I went to the brook and filled my cup, which I set on the hot ashes of the campfire, and then returned to the running creek to scrub my teeth and throw a little water in my face.

Feeling refreshed, I watched my rippling reflection in the stream. My life had dramatically changed during the last few days. I had gone from a freelance puff-piece writer at a third-rate weekly newspaper to whatever it was that described me at that moment. My life had revolved around boring interviews with research and development personnel at companies that only interested my ad-conscious boss to traveling through time, being breath-blasted by a banshee and petting a dragon on the nose. The prior week I was thrilled to cheer long-dead cowboy stars as they shot it out with long-dead villain actors in black and white on the big screen. That had changed to riding into a bright-green, ghost-filled forest with a thought-to-be-long-dead screen cowboy as we shot it out with heavily armed real villains and only survived because of our flying, scaly, reptile backup. And, I believed I was falling in love with the most beautiful woman in the world. Yep. Things had changed.

"IS IT THAT TIME ALREADY?"

I returned to the fire and sat down on my log.

"I could go for a cup of coffee," Sky said, as she walked up behind me with her sleeping bag bundled in her arms. Then, as I quickly tried to grab the cup from the ashes, she handed me a handkerchief and added, "Don't burn yourself, Dave."

I used the cloth to protect my fingers while picking up the metal cup of hot water by its handle. I dumped a packet of instant coffee in it and stirred it with a stick as the beautiful blonde sat down next to me on the log.

"No use heating up another cup," she said. "Let's just share this one."

She also pushed half of her sleeping bag over my legs and snuggled in close.

I didn't say anything, as my jaw was hanging, my words were jumbled in my brain and I was doing my best to keep a mysterious lump from rising on my side of the sleeping bag.

"You were really something out there tonight," she said.

"You're really something right now," I struggled to say.

"I have to admit, the craziness of everything that's happened in the last few days has bothered me as much as anyone else," she confessed. "But I'm beginning to see our little dysfunctional group as a well-oiled team."

I kind of understood what she was saying.

"And, although we have a Hollywood cowboy star with us, as far as I'm concerned, you turned out to be the white-hatted hero."

I felt like blushing and saying "Garsh!" like an old B-western cowboy might say to a pretty schoolmarm after saving her ranch. But instead, I looked into her beautiful blue eyes and moved toward her for a kiss. And I almost made contact when I heard the professor clear his throat behind us.

"It looks like I'm not the only one awake this early," Zack said. "That coffee looks good."

"Let me gather some of the cups from your saddlebags," said Irene, who had just appeared in front of her tent. "I'll make us all some coffee."

Oh, great! I thought. Then, because I was already halfway there, I quickly planted a kiss on Sky's cheek. "More to come," I said.

"Works for me," she responded.

"You folks are pretty darn noisy for night campers," Buck said, while standing up in front of his pup tent and stretching his arms. "And I think I heard somebody mention coffee."

If there were any critters in the area still trying to get a little sleep, they were in for a disappointment. The sounds of guitar pickin' wafted over the campsite as Jimmie Rodgers' voice belted out, "Good morning captain!" and continued on through a complete performance of "Mule Skinner Blues." The quiet and, possibly, romantic morning atmosphere had rapidly become a clattering gaggle of fully awake folks enjoying java, beef jerky, cowboy music and friendly conversation as we prepared for our day.

Following a delightful couple of hours of striking our tents and packing up for the trail, we doused the fire and removed all traces of our campsite. The horses were saddled and ready to go as we rolled up the picket line. Bob seemed happy to begin our return trek. Zack and I were just about to mount up when I turned to say something to Buck.

"Ouch!" I hollered. "What the hell, Bob?"

The equine asshole had bitten me on the butt again.

"He bit me!"

"Actually, Dave," Buck said. "He picked your pocket."

Bob stood there with my wallet in his mouth.

"Do you carry a carrot in that wallet?" Sky asked.

I reached over and snatched my wallet back and showed its contents. "No. I've got my license, credit cards, some cash and this lucky coin."

"Let me see that coin," Zack said.

I placed my new Hopalong Cassidy Lucky Coin in his hand. He thoroughly inspected it, then tossed it on the ground and stomped on it with his boot heel.

"What're ya doin'?"

The professor picked the smashed coin off the soil and held it up.

"That's not a coin," he said, showing that it had come apart with two sides. Some very fine wires and a small chip hung from its insides. "This is a Global Positioning System tracker!"

"Holy crap! That guy at the Retro Theatre."

"Yep," Buck offered. "He gave you something he knew you wouldn't throw away."

"Apparently our enemy has done some fast research on you, Dave," Zack said. "But now we have a lead. When we get back, you can give a complete description of the guy to the feds."

"He said his name was Ben."

"You think he gave you his real name?" Irene asked.

"Nope."

I scratched Bob's ears and nose before mounting up. "Thanks, Bob. That's good detective work. You're certainly smarter than I thought."

Then, as I climbed into the saddle, I believe he tried to bite me again

By getting an early start, we figured we'd arrive at the ranch by ten, which would allow us to clean up and then load up in the Ford and be back in Torrance by four. Of course, considering everything that had happened, that was an optimistic scenario.

And although Irene McCroy couldn't see Lucky, she rode right next to the horse with the "empty" saddle, all the while carrying on an interesting conversation.

"So owls don't gather in large groups and start screaming?" I heard her say.

"Nope," Lucky responded.

"Dragons are good?"

"Yep."

"And Wailing Banshee Ranch is named after real wailing banshees?"

"Yep."

"But banshees don't harm people," she said.

"Nope. They warn people."

"So apparently you've heard the screams before?" I asked.

"Yes. The area is known for them."

"When was the last time you heard them?"

"Just before you folks arrived."

"Obviously," Lucky said, "you were being warned of impending danger—meaning us."

"Are you going to try to explain any of this to Chet?" I asked.

"I'm gonna try."

"This'll either make it easier for you or lead to you being incarcerated in the Looney Tunes Asylum For Wacky Folks," Lucky stated, as he reached over and tapped the lovely ranch owner on her shoulder.

"Well, I'll be damned!" she exclaimed.

"After we're gone, you'll still be able to see the tribal spirits, dragons, banshees and, possibly, other unique entities," Lucky explained. "You'll be forewarned of trouble and able to adjust. Just remember to keep your ability under your hat, as no one in their right mind these days will believe you."

"Thank you, I think."

The trees were enjoying sunlight by the time we arrived at the waterfalls where we stopped on the way out. The timing was perfect as we topped off our canteens, watered the horses and visited the "restrooms."

"Be careful, Sky," I said. "I hear there are some man-eating chuckwallas in the area."

She winked at me and meandered into the trees.

Zack ambled over to me. "You know we are probably still in real danger."

"Yeah, I kind of figured that out," I said. "Any outfit that would take the time to research my background is certainly crossing every T and dotting each I. That means the squad that we dealt with last night was just the first wave."

"And, with helicopters and armed mercenaries, they're spending big bucks to get at us," the professor said. "That tells me we may not just be dealing with a competing R&D firm. We may be up against a large consortium of organized criminals and terrorists, or even a foreign power."

"Well, it sure looked to me last night like they wanted to kill us. You'd think they would rather capture us, or at least you, to get whatever information they could."

"Maybe that's what they were trying. And when things started going south, they grabbed Sky. She's really quite brilliant and has been involved with all of my most important research."

I thought about that a moment, then said, "We better saddle up and get back. I'll go check on her."

I walked to where I last saw Sky and called her name. There was no answer. I walked farther and found her bayonet lying on the ground behind a tree. Frantically I hollered and searched. Nothing.

"She's gone!" I told my friends. "Someone's got her!"

"Mount up!" Buck ordered. "Keep your weapons ready. The enemy's out there!"

"Let's ride to the ranch!" I said. "It's the closest vehicle access to the area."

Lucky handed his reins to Zack. "Take my horse. I'm going up to see whatever I can. I'll catch up with you and let you know what I've found." With a flash of light and the power of dragon wings, Lucky vanished into the sky.

Buck took the lead for the rest of us as we galloped toward Wailing Banshee Ranch. Irene followed in right behind him while leading Sky's horse and Zack came in third with Lucky's horse in tow. I brought up the rear on Bob with one hand on my AR-15, which held a banana clip with a round in the chamber.

Fear washed through my body as my brain told me somehow I had really screwed up. I felt like I had failed Sky, who had quickly become the most important person in my world. After years of struggling with my writing career and never making any lasting relationships, I had found the love of my life—someone who I felt could be my reason for living. The only thing that kept me moving forward was the desperate hope that I could find her and rescue her from the enemy.

Dust and pebbles flew into my face during our frantic rush toward the ranch. Those Morgan horses stood up under incredible stress during the ride. Finally Buck lifted his right hand and slowed to a stop.

"Let's picket 'em here," he said. "We're almost to the ranch and we don't want to ride into an ambush."

Quickly we tied a new picket line. I poured a handful of water for Bob to wet his whistle. Our saddles, bags and bedrolls were placed near the line.

"Put your ammo in your jacket pockets," Buck said. "If our enemy troops are anything like the ones that hit us last night, they've set up a perimeter around the ranch buildings. We'll move in on foot until we are near enough to observe. Then, we'll do whatever it takes."

"Whatever it takes to do what?" Irene asked.

"Whatever it takes to rescue Sky, Chet and your staff," I said. Then I added with a snarl in my voice, "If they are there and still alive."

We moved forward quietly with Buck on point and me coming in second. We kept ten to fifteen feet between us as Irene followed me, and Zack brought up the rear. At about four hundred yards from the structures, Buck led us to some high ground. Among the rocks, we found a decent vantage point where we could see the ranch house and its surrounding buildings.

"There's another one of those gyroplanes," Buck announced.

An unmarked military helicopter sat not too far from Zack's Ford and a few ranch vehicles. The ranch seemed deadly quiet. Smoke drifted up from two chimneys, one from the main-house living room and one on the bunkhouse, telling us there were people inside. I told myself to have faith that Sky was there, and alive. But no humans were visible.

And, speaking of visible humans, Lucky walked up behind us.

"They're all inside," he said.

"And Sky?" I asked.

"She was scooped up by two scouts," he said. "They put her on the helicopter and brought her back here. She's inside too."

I gasped a sigh of relief.

"Any idea who or how many we're up against?" Buck asked.

"There are a total of six men and one woman packin' heat down there," Lucky answered. "I took a little walking recon of the buildings and outside perimeter while I was waitin' for you folks to get here. The staff is tied up and guarded by the woman and one other thug in the bunkhouse. Chet and Sky are in the main house with the other five terrorists."

"Terrorists?"

"Yep," Lucky explained. "These are nasty people. I haven't heard yet who's payin' them. But they're here to capture Zack and take him and Sky to some basecamp for interrogation. They also plan to use them to access Sundance Labs. Once they have Zack, their plan is to kill all of the rest of us before they leave the mountain."

"Any idea where they're from?"

"Their English isn't bad, so they're probably homegrown assholes," Lucky said.

"And there aren't any thugs outside on perimeter guard?"

"Nope," said Josh Randall. "But I noticed they had placed several trip-wired grenades in the brush."

"Good," I said. "I'll remove the wire and re-crimp the pins on a couple. We can use them."

"Too late, Dave," Lucky pointed to four grenades next to a rock. "I already did that."

I grabbed two of them and shoved them in my pocket.

"Buck. Take the other two. You, Lucky and I will go crash their party. Zack, you stay up here with Irene. If you see any of the enemy try to get to the helicopter, shoot them."

"With pleasure."

With our pistols on our hips and our rifles in our hands, Buck and I bent low to the ground and scurried down toward the buildings. A couple of times we had to drop into the dirt and low-crawl infantry-style. Our invisible pal walked standing up straight right next to us. Thick brush covered our advance as we made our way right up to the back of the barn.

"There's nobody in there," Lucky said.

The back barn doors were slightly opened where we could see inside. All was clear. The three of us entered the structure, which only contained a barn cat and two horses in their stalls.

"Irene said she kept crossbows out here," I said.

"Over here," Buck announced.

Three crossbows were mounted on the wall next to a shelf containing three quivers that held five short arrows each. The bows were all metal with pistol grips, slings and scopes. I took one and, using the sling, strapped it over my back. And I tied one quiver onto the left side of my pistol belt next to my bayonet.

"We may need a quick, quiet kill," I said.

Buck nodded, as he twisted one of the hay hooks, which he found hanging along the wall near some bales, up through his belt.

"Now let's see what we can do in the bunkhouse," Lucky said. "I'll just glide in there and check things out. Watch and learn."

The three of us skulked our way out of the barn and around to the back of the bunkhouse. I took off my Stetson and peeked into a window, which was open about three inches at the bottom of the sill. Four cowhands and a man wearing a kitchen apron were gagged and tied up on the floor. A rather rough looking woman with short black hair, wearing leather pants, a camouflage shirt and a holstered Colt 1911 .45 caliber pistol, stood looking down at the hobbled victims. Seated in a chair not far from miss leather-britches was an overweight, fatigue-wearing commando with a perpetual sneer on his fat face. He held his revolver in his hand while leering at his not-so-feminine partner.

Our standing invisible assistant tipped his Stetson, winked and, right in front of us, morphed into a long thin snake. I couldn't help myself as I backed away from the scaly creature, which stuck its head into the window and slithered up the wall and completely inside the bunkhouse. Buck placed his hat on the ground next to mine so we could both look in through the window.

Although he was invisible to all of the occupants of the room, we could see our snake friend reform into Josh Randall standing not far from the enemy couple. With a big silly grin on his mug, he waved at us, pointed at his own face and then moved his hand back and forth in front of the seated thug's eyes as if to say, "Hey. They can't see me." I was never sure exactly what Lucky really was, except for the part about him being a gigantic ham.

The camouflaged thug stood up and walked behind his female partner toward a bottle that stood on a table. Quickly, Lucky reached out and pinched the brunette on her leather-covered butt, and then stepped back to watch the reaction. She bristled, turned quickly and smacked her co-conspirator across the face.

"You asshole!" she spat.

The slap recipient stepped back and snarled, "What the hell?" as he shoved her with his open palm against her chest. This time her reaction brought her closed fist to his nose, dropping the man to the ground, and causing his pistol to slide out of his hand and across the floor. He rolled to his left and reached for the gun. The woman dropped on top of him with her knees landing in the small of his back, causing a loud groan, which was cut off when she shoved seven inches of her KA-Bar knife into his spine at the base of his neck.

Lucky turned toward us and took a bow, at exactly the same time that I fired the crossbow, sending a short, sharp arrow into the woman's left eye, penetrating her brain and the back of her head. She dropped forward onto her partner's body.

"Damn fine shot," Buck said.

"I was aiming for her heart."

"That was obviously too small of a target," he said. "Keep up the good work."

The hogtied staff members' eyes were bugging out as we climbed into the window.

"We're gonna untie you," Buck said. "But please don't make any noise. We still have to take out five black-hats in the ranch house and rescue Chet and Sky."

We quietly removed their gags and cut their ropes, as several of them whispered, "Thank you." Lucky sat patiently on the chair where the late thug had relaxed.

"Are any of you proficient with crossbows?" I asked.

"I am," the mustached man wearing the apron said. "I'm Carl, the cook."

"He's right," said a cowhand with spikey hair and a rather twisted grin on his face. "He may cook like Lucrezia Borgia, but when he gets a crossbow in his hands, he's a Robin Hood."

The cook growled as I handed my crossbow and quiver to him. "How about the rest of you guys?"

"Big Dan and Geezer are also pretty good," the spikey cowboy said.

"Okay," I explained, turning to the oldest guy and the biggest cowboy and said, "Big Dan. Geezer. I want…"

"Who you callin' Geezer?" the old guy said. "I'm Henry. That's Geezer over there!" He pointed to a skinny kid who had to be in his early 20s.

"Hi. I'm called Geezer because I like old movies," the kid said. "And, golly, but you look like Buck Jones."

"I get that a lot," Buck said. "I'm Charlie Roberts."

The largest cowboy looked at me and smiled. "You were right about me, though. I'm Big Dan."

"And I'm Slick," said the man with the spiked hair.

"Good," I said. "I'm Dave Custer. There are two more crossbows with quivers in the barn. Geezer and Dan, grab them. Slick, you and Henry take your former guards' pistols. I want all five of you to take up positions in the brush and be prepared to take out any of the bad guys that step outside. Irene and Zack are up the hill ready to do the same thing. Charlie and I will enter the house and see if we can flush a few of them in your direction."

Of course, Lucky would accompany Buck and me into the ranch house. I figured it would be safer, and quieter, for just the three of us to enter the facility, while the cook and cowboys covered the outside. They were already fortunate just to be alive. I didn't need to involve them in a blazing gun battle inside the building.

Once I got our pistol-and-crossbow-packin' backup situated in the brush, the three of us made our way to the back of the house. We decided we'd take the backdoor into the kitchen area.

"Give me a minute to do another walk-through," Josh Randall said.

"You've got to be the best damned scout in the business," Buck complimented the wraith.

The back door opened just slightly as an invisible, but still creepy, snake slithered inside. After a very long few minutes, Lucky appeared next to us.

"Sky and Chet are tied up and lying on the floor in a corner of the living room," Lucky explained. "It looks like Chet was knocked around a bit, probably during an interrogation."

"What about the thugs?"

"Four of the assholes are in the living room near the windows. The fifth guy is in the kitchen, takin' a nap."

"That's a bit odd."

"Not really," Lucky added. "He just looked very tired, so I bashed him in the head with the butt of my mare's leg."

"You are the most compassionate specter I know," I said.

"Lord knows I try."

I opened the back door and we entered as quietly as possible. The fatigue-wearing trooper was sacked out under the kitchen table. He had a large bump on his forehead, but he was still breathing.

Buck opened the fridge and removed a bottle of beer. "Now if I only had a church key."

"Just twist the lid," I said. "It'll come off."

"Amazing technology in your modern world," he exclaimed as he took his first swallow of the Pilsner. "Now, how do we take out the other four without getting Sky or Chet hurt?"

"I'm going to plant myself at the opening into the hallway while you need to go back outside and stand to the side of the front door. Lucky. You go in and bonk another one over the head with your mare's leg. I'll start shooting from the hall. If any of them make it to the front door, do your thing, Buck. The one in the kitchen is still alive, so we can interrogate him later. Don't take any chances with the others."

Buck went out the backdoor and low-crawled as close as he could to the building all the way around to the front porch. I left the kitchen and sneaked down the hall toward the living room. Once I got to the end of the hall, I assumed a prone position with my AR-15 and waited for Lucky, who walked into the room and straight up to a tall black man who seemed like he might be the leader of the assholes. He wore fatigues, web-gear sporting grenades and ammo pouches, a leather holster containing an Army .45 and was smoking a short dark cigar. His M16 rifle was leaning against a chair.

Invisible Lucky tapped the gunman on the shoulder, causing him to turn around and face nothing. His eyebrows lifted and a look of surprise started to show on his face just as the butt of Josh Randall's sawed-off Winchester struck him on the side of his head. The smacking sound of wood against skull caused everyone to turn toward the falling man.

As the gunman slammed to the floor, two of the other enemy killers lifted their rifles and took positions at the windows while the third man snarled and aimed his rifle at the hostages. I blasted three 5.56mm rounds through his chest, entering to the side of his armored vest, dropping him directly in front of Sky. The two still-breathing gunmen jumped to their feet and fired in my direction, while I sent off several wild shots at the same time as I scurried backward away from their bullets. One of them, who got the idea it was getting a little too hot in the living room, threw the front door wide and ran out of the house only to be hooked like a blue-ribbon rainbow trout.

Buck had slammed his hay hook into the thug's mouth and yanked, lifting his feet off the ground and swinging him outward off the porch. The hook ripped through the man's cheek, tearing his mouth into a double-sized monstrosity and letting him flip out to land on his back in the dirt, his untied vest hanging to the side. Torn and bleeding, he rolled over and jumped to his feet with his bleeding lower lip hanging down below his chin, and faced Buck with his rifle in his hands. With lightning speed, Buck drew his pistol, only to see three crossbow arrows protrude from the man's chest.

The final terrorist ran to the door, just in time to see his rip-faced comrade skewered by the arrows. Finding himself between a Buck and a hard place, he tossed his rifle and placed his hands behind his head. I shoved the barrel of my AR-15 into his lower back and ordered him to his knees and the standard POW position. Buck held his pistol barrel to the back of the man's neck while I went to cut Sky and Chet free.

"Are there any more of you?" Buck asked the asshole.

"Not here."

"Good enough," Jones said, while nudging the dirt-bag with his pistol. "Now, I want you to keep silent for a while. If you make any noise, I will kill you. We find out you lied, I will kill you. And when we interrogate you, you will answer every question truthfully, or I will kill you. Do you understand your rights in this situation?"

"Yes."

I released Sky first and then Chet, at the same time I said, "Zack and Irene are safe. They're both in the rocks waiting for our signal. Carl, Henry, Geezer, Slick and Big Dan are also safe out in the shrubs."

"What about the rest of these bums?" Chet said, as he stepped around the kneeling POW.

"There's one in the kitchen takin' a nap," I said, "and two more stinkin' up the bunkhouse. They're not sleeping."

Sky slowly walked up, placed her head against my shoulder and hugged me tight enough that I could feel her every muscle shaking. "You're fine now," I assured her. Yet she hung on and focused her tear-filled blue eyes on my own. "I could get used to this," I added.

"That's a plan," she said, while placing her lips softly against mine. Thank God we were not wearing body armor, I thought as I held her as close as possible.

"Now you're batting a thousand," Buck said.

Chet went outside and started waving and hooting for everyone to come on down. Carl the cook was the first to appear. He, Big Dan and Geezer checked out the punctured man lying in the dirt. "Nice," Geezer said. "My arrow took out his heart while you two nailed his lungs."

"Like hell," Dan said. "That's my arrow in the center!"

Carl just shook his head and walked up to Buck. "You did a good job hookin' that guy," he said. "He was a mean one. But I'm glad he tore loose so we could puncture his ego."

Henry and Slick arrived with their pistols stuck in their belts. Then Zack and Irene made it down to the ranch house. Sky released me to hug Zack while Chet and his wife had a tearful reunion.

"Henry," I said. "There's a thug sleeping in the kitchen. Would you and Slick please drag him into the living room? We wouldn't want him to wake up and try to get away."

"Sure thing, Dave," the old timer said.

"Geezer. Do you think you and Big Dan could tie up this dick-wad and toss him in the corner? Once Henry and Slick bring in his pal, both he and the other thug that decided to take a nap need to be hogtied as well."

"Gotcha," Big Dan said.

"Carl," Chet said. "It would be nice if you could rustle up some cold chicken and beer for our guests?"

"You bet," Carl responded. "I'll set the two picnic tables with potato salad and beans as well."

"And bring enough for you and the boys," I added. "We all need a little bite and a couple of beers."

Zack motioned for Buck, Sky, Lucky and me to step away from the crowd.

"I've got to let the feds know what happened here," he said. "All these bodies are going to be evidence, but also they're going to cause us grief."

"Before you call Uncle Sam, let's have a bite and a couple of beers to wind down," I said. "And also, we need to interrogate those three assholes in the front room before the government shows up and supplies them with rights and lawyers."

"I already told the one who surrendered what his rights were," Buck said.

"But even if we do get the information we need out of them, once we turn them over to the feds they'll end up charging us with crimes," Sky explained the realities of the 21st Century. "You've all read about soldiers being sent to Leavenworth because of non-uniformed enemy troops' claims of harassment; Terrorists caught creating bombs to kill innocent Americans at home being provided with expensive prima-donna attorneys by the ACLU and other pro-communist groups; violent felons being cut free because they claimed they weren't warned that telling the truth could put them in prison."

"Yes our combination elected officials/attorneys have legislated enough poison pills in the justice system to eliminate the justice part," Zack said.

The pretty blonde added, "It's too bad there isn't a third party who could take them off our hands."

I looked at Lucky and we both got the same idea at the same time.

"Good idea, Sky," I said. "I think we have the perfect solution."

I asked Lucky to put the word out concerning our situation. He smiled and winked.

Big Dan and Geezer did an amazing job of hogtieing the three clowns to the point that they not only couldn't move, they were having a hard time just breathing.

Buck took Henry and Slick back on the trail to fetch the horses. During their way back they stopped off at the stock tank to give our mounts all a good drink before bringing them to the barn, where I met them to help out. We stacked the saddles and blankets on rails, and settled the horses in their stalls with extra helpings of barley. I gave Bob a nice brushing and forgave him for the nipping. He seemed fine with that.

Then all of us went inside to use the indoor plumbing for washing up and other things. Carl, Chet and Irene had set two of the yard's picnic tables with big trays of cold chicken, bowls of beans and potato salad and several pitchers of beer. It looked like everyone was impatiently awaiting us so they could dig in. Lucky, who relished his invisibility, had already consumed a couple of drumsticks, a scoop of potato salad and at least one glass of beer by they time we arrived.

We sat down, lifted our glasses into the air and toasted our survival. Then the laughing, talking and eating began. I scooped a good-sized helping of potato salad along with a breast of chicken onto my plate while Sky topped off my beer glass.

"It must be the fresh mountain air that makes me feel so good," Zack said with a drumstick in his hand.

"That and the fact that we're all still alive," Sky added.

A good-hearted argument returned between Carl, Geezer and Big Dan as to whose arrow struck in the center of Buck's hay-hooked thug.

"I know it was mine," Carl said, "because I'm the best shot with a crossbow."

"I think the best shooting of all was when Dave took out miss leather britches," Buck said.

"Yeah," Carl added. "And she was a snotty shrew!"

"I still wonder why she and that other slug got into a fight," Geezer said. "That was odd. But the timing was perfect."

"I guess it was just a *Lucky* occurrence," Buck said.

We all continued to recount our adventure while enjoying the chow and beer. Sky told me how she was captured and whisked off into the woods by two of the men. She said she was tossed into the helicopter and returned to the ranch. The woman had piloted the chopper.

I noticed Lucky had left the table and found a comfortable spot to lean against a tree stump. Let's get this party started, I thought, as I picked up a bucket and walked over in front of our invisible buddy, winked and placed it face down. Then I announced, "I think we need some music. Now under this bucket is a modern piece of technology that can play any song you can name."

Lucky smiled, his guitar appeared and he awaited his first request.

"There isn't anything under that old wooden bucket," Chet said.

Irene winked at me and told her husband to "Give it a shot. Just request a song."

With a very skeptical expression on his mug, Chet said, "I'd like to hear 'Back in the Saddle Again,' by Gene Autry."

Lucky's guitar strummed and Autry's voice sang, seemingly coming from the upside-down bucket. Chet looked surprised and the cowboys smiled and yipped, while everyone else turned with their beers in their hands and faced the bucket. Just to stir things up a bit, I requested Al Jolson's version of "April Showers." And the voice of the "World's Greatest Entertainer" serenaded our eclectic gathering.

Geezer then yelled out a request for Tex Ritter's "Ballad of High Noon." And immediately the deep voice of the late John Ritter's father sang, "Do not forsake me, oh my darlin'." I'm sure the ranch hands were amazed at the available repertoire of instant classics. But what was really amazing was, to the five of us who could see him, Lucky changing into each entertainer as he performed their songs. He went from guitar-strumming cowboy Gene to Jolie dropping to one knee while emotionally belting out his ballad, and then laid-back Tex Ritter singing probably the most famous western anthem of all.

The icing on the cake was when Big Dan asked to hear "Whole Lotta Shakin' Goin On" sung by Jerry Lee Lewis. Sky, Irene, Zack, Buck and I smiled as a piano appeared next to the tree stump, while Lucky became the blond-haired, wild-man rocker in a white jumpsuit and two-toned shoes. The song rocked. The piano work was amazing. And, at the end, Lucky kicked the stool a good dozen feet from the tree.

I walked over and picked up the bucket.

"It's been fun," I said, "but we've got to interrogate our guests."

Irene, Chet, Carl and Geezer began to gather the dishes and take them to the kitchen. I pulled Big Dan and Slick aside and asked them if they'd mind dragging all of the bodies over behind the barn. "That'll make it easier to clean

THE SONG ROCKED. THE PIANO WORK WAS AMAZING

up the mess inside."

Buck, Zack, Sky, Lucky and I went to face our prisoners. Those of us visible to the men stood directly in front of them, while Lucky ripped off their gags. That shook them up just a tad.

"Let's start with an easy one," I said. "Your names and your parts in this violent little scenario."

All three of the men furrowed their brows and spat without answering. Then, our invisible enforcer punched each of them in the face.

"What the fuck?" the slime-ball, who had so willingly surrendered to save his life, gasped.

Lucky shoved wadded-up rags in the other two thugs' mouths and wrapped towels tightly around each of their faces.

"Now, asshole," I continued. "You may have noticed you are out of your league. So, your name and your rank!"

The man had unkempt, ratty black hair, a complexion that looked like he scrubbed his face daily with a diseased porcupine, a growing bruise on the side of his face and an expression on his ugly mug like a homely seven-year-old princess who just saw her kitten dive into a running wood chipper.

"I'm Danker, Will Danker," he sputtered. "I'm just a working man. Adams is the boss!"

The hogtied black man snorted through his gag and sent mental darts toward Danker.

"Okay, Wanker," I said. "Why are you here?"

"We had orders to capture the two scientists, Delaney and Blue," he said. "The rest of you were to be killed."

"Who sent you?"

"The organization."

"Who are they?"

"They pay us."

"You're mercenaries?"

"No!" He looked like I had insulted him. "We're soldiers of the People's Brigade!"

"Aren't you the assholes who turn protests into riots," I asked.

"We do whatever it takes to defend the people against the fascists!"

"You shoot people who use their 1st Amendment rights to profess their support for the 2nd Amendment!" Sky added.

"The Constitution is a club used against the people by the oppressors!"

Buck stepped forward and gripped the thug by his face. "The Constitution doesn't limit the people in any way. The Constitution limits the government from legislating away citizens' rights, shit for brains!"

"They're fucking commies!" Zack said.

"Yeah," I responded. "But who runs the 'organization' that is paying them?"

"Gag him back up, Lucky," Buck said. "Let's see what one of these other bums has to say."

With no gentleness added, Lucky re-gagged Danker then ripped the gag off the other white commie. This one sported a 1950s crew cut, a broken nose and missing front tooth.

"Name."

"Smith."

"Full name."

"Just Smith."

"Okay, Just Smith," I said. "What's your story?"

"I'm just an anti-fascist community worker."

"You kill people."

"For the betterment of a new world."

"So you're just another violent commie justice warrior?"

"Yeah, you Nazi!"

Buck smacked him. "You realize Hitler's Nazis were socialists."

"No they weren't! They were fascists!"

"Nazi is short for Hitler's National Socialist Party," Buck explained, with one hand around the enemy troop's throat. "Fascism is just a term for a centralized dictatorial government that owns everything and gives orders to their followers. The exact same description fits communist, socialist dictatorships as well."

"Don't waste your time trying to teach history to this waste of oxygen, Buck," Zack said. "Brain-dead thugs like him are beyond learning anything."

"Who's involved with the organization you work for?" I asked.

"I get my orders from Adams! He is our leader."

I nodded to Lucky, who re-gagged Smith and then ripped the gag off of Adams.

"Full name, Adams," I said.

"Devin Adams," the black soldier spat.

"Who gives you your orders, and your pay?"

"I'm not going to tell you shit! I have rights!"

"Actually, you don't have any rights," I explained. "You see, we're not cops, feds or even military. And we are not going to supply you with a crooked attorney or anything else. You will answer our questions or we will kill you. Understood?"

"That ain't the way it's supposed to work!"

"Do you really believe you have the right to kill innocent people for your little revolutionary bullshit and then, when you get captured, demand your rights under our system?" I asked. "You're going to answer our questions or I will break some bones, cut off some non-lethal portions of your anatomy and anoint you with a world of pain until you change your mind."

Lucky used an invisible knife to slice Adams' left ear in half as a virtual exclamation point.

"Jeeze! Okay! I get our pay envelopes and directives from Prof. Ward Winston!"

Zack pulled his phone out and typed in Winston's name for a Google search.

"Prof. Ward Winston is a political activist who teaches claptrap-commie classes at Berkeley. It looks like the tenured asshole has been quite active in the rioting, looting, firebombing movement that our elected fools keep calling 'peaceful protests.' Here's his picture."

I was somewhat shocked to see the social-activist community organizer smiling at the camera in his mug shot exactly the way he smiled at me when he gave me the Hoppy coin in the Retro Theatre.

CHAPTER TEN
CRACK SHOTS AND JACKPOTS

"Holy crap!" I said. Then I explained my reaction to the others.

"That information helps a lot," Zack said, as he started to make a call. "I'll just report in to the feds and let them know to pick up Winston."

I placed my hand on his phone. "I don't think the G-men need to know about our problems here in the Hualapai Mountains."

"What about the bodies?"

"I've asked Lucky to contact his cousins to see if they could swing by."

"You mean…?"

I pointed up to where we could see two large green dragons diving toward the ground somewhere behind the barn.

"Cleanup on aisle five," I smiled.

"What about the helicopter?"

"All of the illegal fully automatic weapons and grenades are loaded in the chopper," I explained. "Our Jack-of-all-trades wraith is going to fly it to a high altitude above a very remote area in the mountains and use one of those grenades to blow it up."

"And how does he survive?"

"Dragon wings."

"Oh. And what do we do with the three hogtied commie stooges in the living room? If we turn them over to the feds, we're in trouble. But we can't just kill them!"

"Oh, no. We're not going to do either. But we can turn them over to some folks who might just teach them a lesson or two."

I went to my room and jumped into the shower. Once bathed, shaved and in clean clothes I felt truly refreshed. While I was brushing my teeth, I heard the helicopter take off. I packed my bag and returned to the living room where I met up with my friends, who were ready to travel.

"You folks know it's best for all of us that no one says anything about what took place," I said to Chet, Irene, Carl and the cowboys.

"We won't say a word," Irene said. "And I hope you all can come back when things are a bit more peaceful."

"None of us will say anything," Geezer said.

"I suggest you cowboys wear western-style pistols," I said. "The guests will expect it of you, and it's always best to prepare to defend yourselves and your brand. There are still quite a few black-hatted varmints out there."

"We'll all be packin' heat," Irene said, "just in case." Then she winked. "If danger does come knockin', I think I'll recognize the warning signs."

Lucky stepped in through the open front door, smiled and I knew the helicopter was gone for good. I looked at our three bound killer commies and laughed to myself.

"Let's get these assholes on their feet," I said.

Buck cut the ropes that hobbled their abilities to walk and removed their gags, while leaving their hands tied behind their backs. We marched them out in front of the building. I asked Irene if she would please take Chet, Carl and the cowboys inside and give us a little privacy.

"Although I believe we would be completely justified," I said to the three commie stooges, "we've decided not to kill you. We, and our friends, are going to open your eyes to knowledge that there is more to life than just your narrow, evil, murderous ways." I turned to Lucky. "Enlighten these assholes, Lucky."

Our friendly neighborhood time-traveling wraith walked in front of the three men and, one by one, tapped them on the shoulder—bestowing them with the ability to see him. Bug-eyed and confused, each of the men seemed shocked to see Steve McQueen as Josh Randall appear.

"We'd like you to meet Lucky," I said. "He's a spirit who has been around longer than time itself."

"And you ain't seen nothin' yet!" Lucky added.

All three men fell back on their butts as a swirling white mist dropped around them, slowly forming into a horrifying shroud-wearing, sharp-toothed, grizzled old crone with long fingers and empty white eyes. The banshee's huge mouth almost stretched over the fools as she screamed her death warning, then vanished into the sky.

"That was a banshee," I calmly lectured. "And now you have been warned."

A dozen hard-eyed, brown-skinned, loincloth-wearing, tribal warriors stepped out of the brush around us. Some held spears. Others had long knives.

"These warriors are the tribal spirits of the forest," I said. "They protect the land, animals and all that's good in nature. Right now, you are not good. But you will be going with them. You will do what they want you to do, or, well, you've seen 'The Searchers,' right?"

"You m-mean they would t-torture us?" Danker stuttered.

"Or worse," I said. "You just got the banshee's death warning. If I were you I'd go quietly."

"Oh, and if you are able to achieve the impossible and escape from these gentlemen," Buck said with a wicked smile. "There's another fate you may want to avoid."

He pointed for the commies to look behind them. Sitting on its enormous hind legs, a huge winged dragon lowered its scaly head very close to their faces, opened its fang-filled mouth and roared, causing small chunks of flaming spittle to spatter around the stooges' feet.

"Dragons don't normally eat people," Buck said. "But, as of this Christmas season, they've found commies to be delicious."

With chattering teeth, tears running down their sweaty faces, puddles of urine soaking into the ground around their fatigue pants, the three killers looked like they were well on their way to insanity. My forest warrior friend smiled and nodded toward me. Then he and his tribe took possession of the three fellow travellers and faded back into the woods.

"I believe justice has been served," Buck said.

"Let's load up the Ford and head for Torrance," I announced. "It's gonna be dark pretty soon, so I'd like to get off this mountain while we can still see."

Ten minutes later we were comfortable in the classic station wagon, bouncing down the rural road toward "civilization."

"By the way," I said. "When do we get paid?"

"You already were," Zack said. "Direct deposit."

"But how did you…? Oh, yeah. You have your ways."

"I called Agent Thorn to see what the status was at the lab," Zack said, while ignoring my financial remarks. "He told me our receptionist had stayed in the facility and that no one else had attempted to breach the building. A guard shift has remained on duty at the entryway to the parking lot. The feds have purged all of our houses, including your place, Dave, of listening devices and there hasn't been any trouble. I told him our vacation had been relaxing even though we cut it short by two days."

"So nothing new to report?"

"Exactly," Zack said. "When we get back, we'll do our own investigation of Prof. Ward Winston and the People's Brigade."

We drove down into the flatland and over to Arizona Highway 95, along the Colorado River separating the state from California and Nevada. Zack went north on 95 to Bullhead City, Arizona, where we could gas up the Ford and stretch our legs. We pulled into a Chevron station, as the professor rightfully believed only the best gas was good enough for his 1940 Ford Deluxe Station Wagon. While the professor pumped the fuel, Sky went into the adjoining mini-mart and bought a bag of chips and a pack of gum.

"It's getting dark," Zack said. "I'm tired. And Laughlin, Nevada, is right across the river. We can get rooms fairly inexpensively at one of the casinos."

"Yeah," I said. "Rooms and food are cheap. Just don't gamble or we'll end up having to take the bus back to Torrance."

"I don't know about you, but my plans are to climb onto a nice soft mattress and get some sleep—with no banshees, dragons, tribal ghosts or commie mercenaries."

"Yep. Casino managers and their enforcers wouldn't allow any of those elements in their buildings," I added. "It wouldn't be good for business."

We continued north on Highway 95 through the small town while munching on Sky's chips. There were several Jet Ski rental companies, a couple of slot machine repair and sales buildings, a head shop and marijuana dispensary, at least two recreational vehicle sales lots among the usual bars, pawnshops and palm and tarot card reading emporiums. Several of the local businesses decorated their parking lots with brightly painted metal statues of desert cactus-like succulents.

Not far from the airport we turned west and crossed a bridge into Nevada. Casinos lined the river on the appropriately named Casino Drive. Several of them had high towers reaching up toward the stars in the clear night sky; certainly the closest most of the gamblers and facility managers would ever get to Heaven. Some had obvious themes, such as a giant riverboat, a crashed flying saucer, a tropical island and a steam-engine train depot. Decisions, decisions, I thought.

Zack pulled the Ford into the parking lot of the Catalina Express Resort and Casino, where we could see dozens of classic vehicles from the 1920s through the '60s gathered.

"It looks like a car show," he said. "We'll fit right in."

Several excited spectators stepped back as the professor parked his wonderful station wagon right in with the assorted Model As, '57 T-Birds,

Studebakers, Cords, Packards and every other marvelous American-made vehicle from the Golden Age of Automobiles. We weren't even out of the Ford before a smiling older couple came up to tell us how beautiful it was.

"Yep," Zack said, as he stepped out of the driver's seat. "It's the only way to travel. Which one of these beauties is yours?"

"The green and white '53 Studebaker Commander hardtop is ours," the man said. "I'm Mike and this is Ella. We've owned it since '63. Bought it for $180."

"You got your money's worth, Mike," Zack said. "I'm Zack, and I've only had the Ford here for the last few years. I hope you folks don't mind that we've kind of barged into your show."

"Not at all! A vehicle like yours is always welcome. We're the Rockin' Wheelies classic enthusiasts."

"There certainly is a lot of quality history sittin' right here on this pavement."

It looked like most of the members were retired, well-off folks who had the time and the interests to enjoy their lives. Some of the men were using buff rags to touch up under their hoods, while others were laughing, slapping backs and drinking bottles of beer. A few of the women who came in the '50s cars wore bobby socks and pedal pushers, while others sported poodle skirts. Quite a few of the men wore caps with their Vietnam War military patches on the front. One heavy set man wearing a suit, tie and fedora looked exactly like Broderick Crawford next to his black and white 1955 Buick "Highway Patrol" police car. The Rockin' Wheelies club was truly the American dream for some people, and I thoroughly approved of their enthusiasm.

"Say, Mike," the professor asked. "Do you think there are any rooms still available here at the Catalina Express?"

"No problem, Zack. This is Laughlin. There are always vacant rooms to be had."

We walked through the gathering on our way to the casino. Buck slowed and appreciated several cars from the 1930s. I looked at a robin's egg blue '56 T-Bird with wide white sidewall tires, a chrome-wrapped continental kit, V-8 engine and removable hardtop and thought maybe I should get one of those instead of a new red Lexus convertible. Invisible Lucky jumped into the driver's seat of a 1954 Chevrolet Bel Air convertible and honked the horn, causing the owner to immediately inspect under the hood to see why his car was honking with no one around. I shook my head and our singing spirit caught up with me.

"Lighten up, Dave," Lucky whispered. "We're at a casino!"

"Where we will do our best to keep a low profile. We're not here to wear funny hats and dance on tables. All of us need a good night's sleep."

"You're no fun."

We entered the resort and walked past several indoor palm trees that fronted a jungle-themed barroom. A well-dressed black man played beautiful music on a piano in a wide area of the walkway that led to the machines. Several people stood around the instrument, laughing, singing and requesting songs from movie musicals. The pianist apparently had the sheet music for every song ever recorded in his large folder, in that he would take the time to look up each request and then amaze his audience with his performances. Sky took my hand in hers and we stopped to enjoy the man's talent for a couple of classic songs. Appropriately enough, he played "Moonlight Becomes You," while the halo-like glow of a Wheel-of-Fortune slot machine bounced off her golden hair.

Zack checked us in and got three rooms on the second floor. Sky got the single, while Lucky and I would share a double, as would Buck and Zack. The professor handed out key cards.

"Who's up for a beer?" Lucky asked.

"Not me," Zack answered. "I'm headed to bed."

"Maybe just one," I said, leading the way into the Fantasy Fern Bar.

I ordered four bottles of Red Ale and carried them to a table where Buck, Sky and Josh Randall were already seated.

"Just don't get into another bar fight," Sky said. "I'm too tired for that."

"And, these places have video cameras everywhere," I added. "Some boys with bent noses are probably watchin' us right now."

"So they might get confused if they saw something strange," Lucky said, as he lifted his beer up and took a big swig.

"Yeah," Buck said. "Like an invisible beer drinker, for instance."

"Oh, shit!" I said. "Drink up. We'll move on."

We left the bar before any curious security types showed up. I saw Mike and Ella feeding a couple of slot machines near the stairs.

"Any luck?" I asked.

"Not yet," Ella said. "But we got time."

"And we've got the money," Mike said. "These are only nickel slots."

Lucky reached over and laid his hand on Ella's machine. Bells started ringing and a cascade of nickels tumbled down into her tray.

"You guys are good luck!" she yelled.

"Yep," said Buck. "Another *Lucky* occurrence."

"Let's hit the sack, gang," I said. Then I whispered, "Before we cause a noticeable situation."

We walked toward the stairs as Lucky tapped two machines within reach that were being played by a couple of World War II veterans in wheelchairs. Bells were ringing, coins were dropping and veterans were cheering as we climbed the stairs to the second floor and made our way to our rooms. Buck entered his first. I stepped into the doorway of Sky's room to say goodnight, for a good five minutes. I wanted it to be longer, but I knew I had better join Lucky before he decided to return to the casino.

The beautiful blonde cowgirl and I held each other tightly and whispered in each other's ears. I wasn't sure exactly what we were saying, but I knew it was wonderful. I thought a water hose might be needed to get us apart, but then I heard Lucky's voice. "You comin'?"

That did it. Sky said, "Goodnight," and closed the door. Lucky and I went on to our room, which contained a small refrigerator, chest of drawers, flat-screen television on the wall and two queen-size beds. I went to the bathroom, washed my face and teeth and used the porcelain convenience. That's when everything that had taken place over the last several days started spinning in my mind, again. Time travel. Transferring bodies. Invisible cowboys. Dragons. Banshees. Tribal spirits. Gunfights. Mercenary commies. I tossed more cold water in my face and returned to the bedroom.

Lucky looked at me and said, "I'm not really tired either. You want to go get a sandwich and another beer?"

"Will you behave if we do?"

"Well, duh," he said, as the room flashed and he appeared as a young Elvis in a ruby studded white jumpsuit with an eagle on the back and a long blue scarf hanging down from his neck. "I'm invisible. Remember?"

My judgment may have been a tad faulty at that moment, but I decided to give it a shot. We headed back downstairs. One good choice was that I left my big white Stetson in the room. The casino already had enough cowboys working the one-armed bandits. If Lucky were visible, he would've fit right in. Every third guy in the place seemed to think he was Elvis. Several had obviously spent hours in front of mirrors trying to swirl their comb-overs into rocker pompadours. A lot of them were wearing big-framed sunglasses, which went with their dated western shirts that stretched tightly over their old-Elvis waistlines.

Other guys sported stereotypical "Texas millionaire" looks with tan Stetsons and inexpensive polyester western jackets with leather-looking plastic elbow patches and big cigars. Many of the women wore their hair in Tammy Wynette hairdos, which contained enough hairspray that I was worried one of the cowboy's cigars might touch one and set off a three-alarm blaze.

I went up to a corner bar and purchased two bottles of Miller Lite. I sipped mine while Lucky gulped his down.

"A fool such as I shouldn't carry my bottle around with me," Lucky Elvis said. "With all the suspicious minds around here, we might get caught in a trap. A-ha-hoo."

My time-traveling pal might be otherworldly. But on this planet, he was just plain bat-shit crazy.

We continued our walk through a "smoking section" of slot machines that was packed with cigarette-smoking gamblers, some sitting in wheelchairs with oxygen tanks strapped to them. The possibility of explosions didn't seem to bother any of the gamblers. The air was thick and carried the essence of tobacco and wet Depends. I looked up to see a large banner hanging from the ceiling that touted one special slot machine that only took twenty-dollar bills. The banner's bold-faced headline read, "Win more gold than there is in William Devane's safe!"

Middle-aged cocktail waitresses wearing swimsuits, net stockings, bright-red lipstick and forced smiles delivered free drinks to the slot gamblers, sometimes receiving tips for their efforts, sometimes having to listen to angry remarks concerning the machines.

In front of the resort's Rain Barrel Lounge was a sandwich-board sign touting, "A special Christmas tribute performance," at midnight, starring "Sunny and Share." I stood there a moment looking at the picture of a tall, skinny man in a long black wig and hip-hugger bell-bottoms (Maxwell "Share" Rosen) and a short, fat woman with a Beatle wig, fake mustache and hippie vest (Candice "Sunny" Weintraub) singing into one microphone.

"The Elvis suit isn't quite as weird as it seemed a few minutes ago, is it Dave?" Lucky said.

"It's still early," I said. "Let's go in here and get another beer and some peanuts."

We went up to the bar where the lighting wasn't very good. Apparently it was karaoke hour, as a large man in a plaid jacket and Levis attempted to sing "Chances Are" with a voice that sounded like Johnny Mathis, if he had a very bad overbite. When he completed the song, at least three people applauded.

"Now this looks like fun," Lucky said.

"Don't even think about going up there!"

A young woman of about thirty stepped up on the stage and whispered in the DJ's ear.

"Cornelia will now sing 'Dream a Little Dream of Me,'" the man said, as he programmed in the background music.

Cornelia didn't seem like the type that anyone wanted to dream about, except for maybe Popeye's friend Wimpy, whose appetite for hamburgers she probably shared. She started off, "Stars shining bright above you," reminding me more of Mama Cass than Doris Day. Her efforts garnered at least four people applauding, including Lucky.

"C'mon, Dave," he said. "Get up there!"

"Absolutely not!"

A laughing, rather tipsy man in his late fifties dragged his companion, a plump bottle-blonde in a too-tight black cocktail dress onto the stage and, with their backs to the audience, told the DJ what they wanted to sing. The grinning computer-age platter spinner turned them around to face the audience, and announced, "Larry Packman and Angel Court will sing 'Jackson,' like Johnny Cash and June Carter!"

I must say they had the moves. If I were completely deaf, I would have said the choreography was amazing. But I could hear, and Cash and Carter, they weren't. I do believe Angel really put her heart in the part of her performance where she sang, "Go play your hand you big-talkin' man, make a big fool of yourself!"

Mercifully, the song ended with a smattering of applause.

"That was amazing!" Lucky said. "It's your turn, Dave!"

"I don't sing, Lucky."

"That's okay. I do. Get up there."

I shook my head, sipped my beer and sat still on my stool. Then, an uncaring, forceful, invisible Elvis, with the strength of a dragon, gripped my arms, lifted me up and carried me to the stage with my legs dangling like a stupid 1950s television marionette. I stood there with my eyes wide and my mouth open under that bright yellow spotlight as the DJ asked me what I wanted to sing. Lucky's hand gripped my jaw and opened it and shut it as he announced in a deep voice, "Cow Cow Boogie." The man typed into his computer and, sure enough, he came up with the background orchestra for the 1941 hit. The piano started things off and, with my jaw opening and shutting via invisible hands, the voice of Ella Mae Morse came out of my mouth singing, "Out on the plains, down near Santa Fe, I met a cowboy riding the range one day."

The audience was dead silent, eyes were wide and drinks were frozen on their way to lips, as I belted out that most embarrassing song in front of total strangers. When I got to the part of, "Comma ti, ii, yi, ay, comma ti, yipply, ii, ay," I started to fantasize a thousand ways to kill Lucky. When the music stopped, the audience was still frozen. Heads began to turn and people looked at each other, then slowly the applause started, and continued until everyone stood up and cheered.

"That was stupendous!" the DJ said. "Here's my card. Call me later. I'll get you a spot with Sunny and Share."

I stumbled my way down off the stage and out the door.

"That was so much fun!" Lucky exclaimed. "Let's go back!"

"You asshole!" I said. I then realized the lady at the first slot machine thought

I was talking to her.

"Get away from me, creep!" she yelled.

My blood pressure was high. My brain scolded me for not staying in my room and going to bed.

"Really, Dave!" Lucky said with excitement on his face. "You could have sung 'Happy Trails' as both Roy and Dale! We could've knocked 'em dead!"

CHAPTER ELEVEN
STREET OF FIRE

woke up the next morning, still angry from the night before.

"Good morning, Dave."

Lucky sat on the edge of his bed and smiled at me.

"Asshole!" I greeted him.

"Now Dave. That's not a good way to start the day. Last night is over and today is a beautiful morning. The sun is shining, sweet little blue birds are chirping and pretty green-headed mallard ducks are enjoying the Colorado River."

"Bite me!"

"Hey. I admit I went a little too far with the karaoke thingy, but that's all in the past. We've got a wonderful day ahead to enjoy our drive back to Torrance."

"You dragged me up on that stage and made me sing like a woman! I felt like Terry Fator's turtle puppet! Except he gets to sing like Roy Orbison. You made me sing like Ella Mae Morse! How could you do that to me?"

"I am so sorry. There were only a few people in the audience and most of them were drunk. No one's going to remember your amazing performance."

"I'll remember it! Forever!"

"Look. Zack, Buck and Sky are already downstairs at the breakfast buffet. They don't know anything about our little adventure last night. Let's just go down and have a nice breakfast with our friends. You'll feel a lot better after some coffee and eggs."

I growled, got up and staggered into the bathroom. A quick shower, shave and other things brought me back to an almost human attitude. I dressed, grabbed my Stetson and went downstairs with the traitorous Lucky following just out of reach. A lot of gamblers had gotten an early start on their slot play and quite a few of them were already holding drinks or bottles of beer.

The Catalina Clambake Buffet was packed, yet we could see Sky and the gang wave as we entered the room.

I walked up to their table just as at least half of the folks in the room began applauding. I looked up to see all the adults standing. They started singing, "Comma ti, ii, yi, ay, comma ti, yipply, ii, ay," as Sky pointed at me and said, "You're the 'Cow Cow Boogie' boy singer everybody's talkin' about?" Then she, and everyone at the table, began to laugh. With the look of an angry wolf on my face, I turned quickly and Lucky was gone.

Buck looked up at me, shook his head and said, "Sit down, Dave. Have some breakfast and then we'll be on our way. What happens in Laughlin stays in Laughlin."

Sky leaned over and bit me on the ear, "Except when I remind you of it again and again. And I definitely will do that." I would have probably been more upset with her; except she was one gorgeous woman—and she did nibble my ear.

I guzzled my coffee and ate a waffle that had to have been made of concrete before standing up and suggesting we hit the road. The nodding confirmed consensus, without editorial comment.

As we left the buffet, I stopped in my tracks. Right in front of me were Sunny and Share, frowning like Yosemite Sam and an angry horse. Standing next to them and pointing at me was the karaoke DJ. Share tossed his head, flipping one side of his long black wig over his shoulder and, in a very deep voice, said, "Scram Bub!" Then Sunny wiggled her fake mustache, glowered up at me, and said in an equally deep voice, "Yeah! We're working this side of the street!"

Sky stepped in front of me and shoved the strange tribute singers to the side so we could walk between them. "And you can have it!" Sky told the performers as she pulled me along.

"Gee, thanks Sky," I said, scurrying up beside her. "At least you've got my back."

"No problemo, Dave," she said. Then she winked at me and added, "I got you babe!"

We checked out of the resort, hopped in the Ford and headed toward the interstate. Zack drove. Buck was in the front passenger seat. Sky and I took up the second bench seat. And whenever I peeked toward the back seat, it looked like Lucky was pretending to be asleep.

Once on Interstate 40, the traffic was minimal. It was another clear, cool day in the desert. There were times that it seemed like we were the only travelers on the highway. That is, until we passed a roadside rest about sixty miles west of Needles. That's when two black Chevy sedans pulled out behind us.

"I think we've picked up a tail," Zack said.

"They must have been waitin' for our very identifiable Ford at that rest area,"

Buck said.

"Well," I said. "We're out in the true middle of nowhere. And if those are People's Brigade vehicles, we're pretty much screwed."

"No were not," the traitorous voice from the backseat said.

"Care to explain, Elvis?" I said, even though the butthead was back in his Josh Randall disguise.

"I brought security," Lucky said, pointing out the window and up.

Pacing our vehicle at about two thousand feet above us were three dragons.

"Punch it, Zack!" Buck said. "I see weapons sticking out of windows!"

The big Ford engine roared as Zack tried to pull away from the tenacious sedans. I opened my window, grabbed my .44 and prepared to return fire. Fortunately, the two enemy-filled sedans lost interest in attacking us at about the same time as they lifted into the air. Invisible talons broke glass and punctured metal while our dragon friends rapidly gained altitude to several hundred feet into the sky, before they released the first black Chevrolet and its presumably terrified occupants.

"Wow!" Buck said, while pointing off into the distance where two vehicles tumbled out of the sky and exploded like Napalm canisters in the barren desert landscape. "I hope those guys used the restrooms back at the roadside rest. If not, they might have embarrassed themselves on the way down."

"It's a good thing our friends are invisible," Sky said. "Otherwise there might be trouble. I don't think NORAD is prepared for those refugees from a Ray Harryhausen movie."

"Ooh, ooh!" Lucky said. "I liked the one with the horned cyclops."

I looked back up into the sky and saw the flying reptiles had returned to their previous altitude of about two thousand feet above us and were once again pacing our speed.

"Are they going to follow us all the way home?" Zack asked.

"Nope," my invisible former friend said. "They'll peel off near San Berdoo. Dragons don't like to get too close to LAX."

The many miles of desert landscape gave me plenty of quiet time to try to purge my irritation toward the invisible turd with the mean sense of humor, and concentrate on my thoughts of a future with the goddess napping next to me with her head on my shoulder. The warmth of her body snuggled against mine was like Heaven, I thought, even though I didn't know that much about her. I wondered if she liked to dance, enjoyed sports or whether she was a cat person or a dog person. I only knew that whatever she liked had to be wonderful, even if she kept a couple of those disgusting, hairball-coughing, furniture-clawing cats.

We hit Interstate 15 and gassed up at Barstow, giving us a chance to stretch

THEY RELEASED THE FIRST BLACK CHEVROLET...

our legs, use the restrooms and have burritos and soda at a Crazy Chicken fast-food joint. From there it was fairly smooth going as we passed through Victorville and dived down the Cajon Pass toward the wall-to-wall Southern California cities.

We had whipped onto the 60 and were driving through Pomona when Zack's cellphone rang. While steering with his left, he used his right to yank the state-of-the-art iPhone out of his shirt pocket and place it next to his ear. "Yeah." He listened, then said "Wilco," and shoved it back in his pocket.

"We have to make a little detour on our way home," he said. "Agent Thorn is going to meet us at one of my subsidiary companies, All-American Electronics in Whittier."

"What's the problem?" I asked.

"That's what we'll find out," the professor answered. "A long-time friend of mine, Norville Dumont, manages the company. Apparently there's a little bit of a situation going on."

"Anything to worry about?" Buck asked.

"I don't think so. But just in case, your weapons are behind the back seat," Zack said. "And remember what state you're in, so no AR-15s or holstered weapons in public. The People's Republic of California frowns on that. Just put on your jackets and hide your pistols and bayonets in your pockets, along with any backup ammo."

"Sounds like nothing to fear but fear itself, except for maybe a reenactment of the gunfight at the O.K. Corral," Buck said.

We pulled off the freeway at Azusa Avenue and then drove over the hills on Colima Road into Whittier. Zack took a right on Mar Vista and continued to Pickering where, once we saw the problem, he decided to pull a couple of blocks away from the electronics company and park in a residential neighborhood.

"I don't need a Molotov cocktail tossed through my window," he said.

I completely understood his reason for avoiding the possibility of damage to that amazing classic Ford Station Wagon. If it were mine, I'd lose my temper every time a bird pooped on it.

Pickering Avenue was crawling with an angry mob of black-clad, masked whiners shaking their fists, screaming and marching in circles in front of All-American Electronics. Some of the so-called "peaceful protesters" were throwing rocks. Others carried signs denouncing the company, the federal government, the military, law enforcement and, I believe, motherhood and apple pie.

"Are those folks Moslems?" Buck asked.

"Maybe some of them," Zack said. "And they're called Muslims these days. But the majority of them are your garden-variety socialist, communist, useful idiots carrying out violent dictates from assholes like that guy!"

He pointed at a man standing on the dented hood of, obviously, someone else's car. He had a bullhorn up to his lips as he screamed at his minions to "bring down the All-American fascists." He didn't look like Vladimir Lenin, Joseph Stalin or even Joy Behar. The screamer was a white-haired older man wearing a Cubs baseball cap and a khaki jacket, which made him look like he could be a western-movie fan who might introduce himself as Ben—even though his real name was Professor Ward Winston.

"There's our boy," Buck said.

"And I'll bet a good number of those masked comrades are members of the People's Brigade," Sky added.

The rioters' rhetoric increased in volume as they had virtually closed off access to the electronics company. A poorly dressed, overweight woman wearing a bandana over the lower part of her face screamed hysterically as she waved an American Flag while waddling to the center of the group. Others began to chant, "Burn it! Burn it!" She placed the symbol of our country on a pile of rags, cardboard, and Starbucks cups in the street, while another grinning, redheaded nutcase, who was wearing a ragged Cheshire cat T-shirt, pulled one of two cans of lighter fluid from his back pockets and began squirting the banner and the other flammable materials.

"We can't let that happen!" Buck said, while reaching into his jacket pocket for his revolver.

Lucky placed his hand on Buck's and said, "Leave it to me, Rough Rider." He then rushed into the throng of "protesters," directly toward the doused flag.

"Somehow, I believe those lunatics are in big trouble," Sky said.

The nut in the striped-cat shirt bent low over the flag pile and struggled with a lighter. Our invisible friend ran up behind him, removed both cans of lighter fluid from the commie's back pockets and started squirting the flammable liquid as he hurried in an expanding circle within the gathering of rioting lunatics. After completing four rings he squirted a trail to the speaker's vehicular platform.

Buck, Zack, Sky and I backed away from the crowd and stood by a boarded-up brick storefront. The gathering of self-righteous mental midgets increased their violent rhetoric as they prepared to offend all common-sense Americans by torching the symbol of our freedom. Several grinning dimwits prepared their phones to video the atrocity.

Finally successful at flicking his Bic, the Cheshire-cat goon lowered his burning lighter toward the American Flag. At the same time, Lucky sped through the crowd, snatched the Flag off of the crackpots' pyre, and rushed to the sidelines. Kitty goon touched his fire to the fluid-soaked cardboard, which burst into flame and sent a quickly moving blaze up his arm and over his back causing him to scream like an Arizona banshee. No one tried to help him, as the fire trail had covered the pants of the woman who brought the flag, leaving her to flap her arms and squeal, and continued throughout the crowd in an ever-expanding radiating circle causing flaming activists to panic, trample and roll over each other, thus leading more socialists to feel the burn. The light show culminated as a lighter-fluid trail flamed up the side of the speaker's platform and into the open gas tank, bringing about a colorful fireworks-like explosion that tossed Prof. Ward Winston a good twenty feet into a pile of manure bags, which his group had carefully prepared for throwing at police officers, if and when officials allowed them on the scene.

"I wish we had brought a six-pack of beer to enjoy during the fireworks," I said, as we watched some of the less-burned activists attempting to put out their comrades. Some of the "victims" continued to scream, some groaned, and a couple even pleaded for their co-conspirators to "call 911!" How ironic, I thought.

Within minutes, sirens announced the arrival of two police cars, a fire truck and an ambulance. A tall, fully uniformed male firefighter ran up to us and asked, "Are you okay?"

"Oh, we're fine," I said. "How are you?"

"Can't complain. Who are these people?"

"The governor would call them peaceful protesters," I said. "I'm not sure why, but they were tryin' to burn an American Flag."

"The traitors!"

"Exactly. They also may have been attempting to emulate the activities of some Vietnamese Buddhist monks from the 1960s, but they obviously weren't very professional about that, either."

"Maybe if they practiced more," he quipped, as he followed four law enforcement officers and three paramedics into the throng of crying, complaining, crispy commies.

"Well guys," a voice behind me said. "I guess we're too late."

I turned and faced three Levi-wearing elderly men with smiles on their faces. One very tall, thin black man with short, thinning, gray hair, wearing a blue baseball cap with a Navy corpsman insignia on it, leaned against a lumpy Irish cane. The other two men wore First Cavalry patches that sported airborne tabs on their caps. One of the Cav vets was a clean-shaven gent with thick white hair and the other was a bald man with a white goatee and a cigar in his mouth.

The cigar smoker said, "What'd we miss?"

"A bunch of dumb-shit commies tried to burn a flag," Buck said. "For them, it didn't end well."

"Dammit!" the tall black man said. "We missed all the fun!"

A large, not-too-bright looking protestor staggered out of the street and advanced toward us with a three-foot pipe in his hands. Two rather sooty, singed sycophants followed behind him.

"What're you assholes lookin' at?" he spat. Then he saw the American Flag that invisible Lucky had quietly passed over to me.

"A street-load of over-cooked dimwits," Buck said.

The man planted his feet in front of Buck Jones and pulled his pipe back like he was ready to hit one out of the park. Then he dropped to his knees as the tall, thin, black man bounced the knotty end of his Irish cane off the top of his head.

"It's a shillelagh," the ex-Navy corpsman said with a practiced Irish lilt. "Sure and 'tis a gift from the Emerald Isle."

One of the dirty sycophants wearing a burnt sweatshirt snarled and ran right at Buck, only to suddenly stop and fall backward as the cowboy's granite-hard fist smashed into his face, causing what looked like it might be some permanent damage. The other swung a board in my direction, but lost interest in the move when the edge of my right hand cracked into his Adam's apple. The two men joined their grumpy comrade on the sidewalk like three lambs huddling together for a nap, one of them continuing to choke.

"Thanks, pal," Buck said to the tall man with the cane.

"My pleasure."

"I'm Charlie Roberts, this is Dave Custer, Zack Delaney and the pretty lady is Sky Blue," Buck did the introductions as we all shook hands.

"I'm Donald Finn, but my friends call me Sharky," the tall man said. "My two Cav-vet buddies are Dan Loman and Patrick Stone."

"It's great to meet all of you," I said. Then I held out the Flag. "This is the American Flag we rescued from those shits. It needs someone to wash the lighter fluid out of it."

"We'd be glad to take care of that," Loman said. "And our retirement facility needs a new banner."

"Great," I said, as I handed it the man. "We're pleased it's found a good home."

"God bless America," Sharky said. "And Merry Christmas."

"And Merry Christmas to you gentlemen, too," I said. "But for right now, we're gonna have to go inside that electronics company. And you guys might want to go somewhere else too, before any elected officials, crooked attorneys or media types show up. When they do, those commie rioters could swiftly become innocent, peaceful-protester, victims of society."

"Yep," Stone said. "Us three geezers better skedaddle before someone decides we're the bad guys, again."

Our three new friends left the scene as we tiptoed through the messy street, making sure not to bother the police officers, paramedics and whiney rioters. The firefighter I had spoken with earlier was peeling what was left of a Cheshire-cat T-shirt off of a swollen, blistered man with clumps of red hair sticking out on top of his head.

"He's the one who tried to light the American Flag on fire," I said to the first responder.

"Then he got what he deserved."

Lucky was standing on the All-American Electronics porch waiting for us. "Those People's Brigade reds sure know how to warm up a party," he said. "Where's Winston?"

I looked over to the pile of manure bags. "He's gone."

"Well that stinks."

"So does he, I'm sure."

We knocked on the door and a tall blond man wearing a suit and tie opened it.

"Agent Thorn," Zack said. "These folks are my Sundance team."

The professor introduced us to the fed and then to the company's manager, Norville Dumont.

"The rioters started showing up this morning," Thorn said. "I don't know what just happened, but they sure messed themselves up."

Lucky sat on the counter and smiled at us.

"They tried to burn a flag and a whole bunch of them caught on fire," Zack said.

"Just another *Lucky* coincidence," Buck added.

CHAPTER TWELVE
KILLING TIME

"We were warned," All-American Electronics manager Norville Dumont said. "I thought it was just a mob-wannabe shakedown."

"You mean some of these street punks had shown up earlier to make threats?" I asked. "What did they want?"

"Two days ago I was called to the front," Dumont explained. "Benny told me a couple of white-collar types wanted to talk to me. When I came to the lobby, two men, both wearing blue suits, ties and looking very businesslike, introduced themselves as representatives of something called the People's Brigade."

"I only found this out this morning," Thorn added.

"They demanded to see the files of everything that I delivered to you, Sundance Labs," the manager continued. "I told them they could climb a tree, or something to that effect. Then one of them shoved me to the floor and said they would destroy the building if I didn't fork over everything, including lists of materials that were used for time travel efforts, of all things."

I looked at Zack, who wasn't happy.

"I didn't think…" I started to say.

"That's a ridiculous demand!" Zack said loudly, cutting off my remark.

"Those two thugs started to slap me around when Benny came back into the room with a shotgun in his hands," Dumont said. Then he turned to Thorn. "We keep it just in case of an attempted robbery."

"Not a problem," the fed said. "Benny did the right thing."

"The two suited shits backed off, while telling us they would return soon to take what they wanted."

"Did you call the police?" I asked.

"I did," the manager answered. "I told them Benny used a baseball bat to send the thugs packing. I knew if I told them about the shotgun, they would have confiscated it."

"Local officials seem to want businesses and citizens to be unarmed," the fed said. "Some of us at the NSA are a little more realistic."

"The cops filled out a report," the manager stated. "But nothing came of it."

"Actually, that report crossed one of our agent's desk this morning," Thorn said. "Because this company is on a list of Sundance properties, I came here immediately. While I was interviewing Mr. Dumont, the crowd of troublemakers began to show up outside."

"It's a good thing you were here," Zack said. "Norville. Did you also report this to Sundance Labs?"

"I certainly did, right away. I called and gave B.C. a complete rundown right after the police officers left."

"Who's B.C.?" Buck asked.

"Beth," Zack said. "She used to work for Norville and, in those days, went by her initials."

My eyes bugged out. I realized where I'd seen the receptionist before. She had accompanied her husband, James Carpenter, J.C., to the awards luncheon where my business article was honored.

"Beth Carpenter," I muttered under my breath.

"Have you ever been threatened like that before?" Buck asked the manager.

"No. It seemed like the strong-arm tactics used by the mob and street gangs in the old days. But, as far as I know, that hasn't been attempted in this neighborhood since the 1970s."

"Agent Thorn," Zack said. "Can you have a couple of feds keep an eye out here for a few days? I think today's rioters will spend a while licking their wounds, but I'm not sure if their handlers will bring in some new thugs to start again."

"I can do that," Thorn answered. "I've got our mobile headquarters not far from your Torrance facility. I'll schedule two agents to be in this neighborhood in case of any more trouble. Like the guards that are posted in front of your facility, they'll work shifts and can keep in contact with our mobile unit."

"Thank you. Sky, Charlie, Dave, we better get back to Torrance."

As we left the electronics building, a few television news crews were taping while city employees cleaned up the street. Two filthy, black-clad, disgusting looking thugs were being interviewed about what they called a "peaceful protest" that became violent when police and firefighters showed up and "attacked the innocent participants." Oh, well, I thought. No good deed goes unpunished.

One of the local talking-head reporters confronted us while her cameraman shoved his machine in our faces.

"Did you witness any of the police brutality?" the overly face-powdered woman said while thrusting her microphone at me.

Lucky moved quickly and, with the finesse of a true magician, dismantled the video recorder while the cameraman held it. We pushed past them as they stood looking at the pieces of their company camera that were spread all over the sidewalk.

"You really should take better care of your equipment," Buck said, as the rest of us laughed at the media mutts.

Once we got back to the Ford and started driving toward Torrance, Sky asked, "How did the suited guys know about time travel?"

"I don't know," Zack said through gritted teeth. "The feds don't even know anything about that. They are aware of our tissue experiments, but time travel efforts have been secret from everyone except Sundance staff. Somehow, our security has been compromised."

"The best way to get to the bottom of this is to get our hands on Prof. Winston," Buck said.

"Zack. Did you know Beth was married to my former publisher?" I asked.

"Beth is divorced," he said. "I believe she had been married to someone in advertising, but they broke up five years ago."

"Then why would she attend an awards luncheon with her husband, James

Carpenter, just six months back? That's the same J.C. who sent me to interview you, as well as other research facilities in the past."

An awkward silence rattled around the interior of the Ford. Someone had leaked information concerning the professor's time travel experiments, I thought. Only Sundance employees knew anything about the laboratory's groundbreaking accomplishments. My former publisher's wife works there and, I pondered, she lied about her marital status. She probably was restricted from getting her hands on research materials, but she certainly would know which other companies were either owned by Delaney or supplied Sundance.

"Well I, for one, have a hard time thinking Beth would compromise the company," Sky said. "She is always so nice and helpful. And her access to classified levels is limited."

"And she's also very pretty," Buck said. "Most of the female traitors from that fiery protest were ugly as mud fences."

"As much as I'd like to agree with you, Buck," I added. "I've found that real-life villains aren't selected by casting directors. Equality works both ways. Some of the most evil people in today's world have been good-looking women. Of course, if they're in Congress too long they do tend to wrinkle up."

"Let's not prejudge," Zack said. "When we get to the labs we'll figure things out."

About forty-five minutes later, we arrived at the Torrance industrial park and stopped at the entry to the Sundance Laboratories parking lot. A tall man with a diagonal scar across his chin, wearing a dark suit and carrying an M16 in his right hand, walked up to Zack's window, looked at the driver first and then the rest of us.

"I'm Agent Watkins. Everything has been very quiet, professor," the man said, as he stepped up onto the running board. "I'll escort you to the building."

We pulled forward and Zack parked directly in front of the facility entrance.

"Do you have your key card sir?" the agent asked.

Zack pulled his sleeve back from his watch and waved his hand near the door. There was a click and the door swung wide. The professor, Sky, Lucky, Buck and I entered the facility with Watkins following. The lobby looked the same, with its wonderful framed movie posters on the walls and Beth behind the counter.

"Welcome home, Zack," the receptionist said.

"Thanks. How're things here?"

"Couldn't be better," she said. "Hi Sky, Dave, Mr. Roberts."

"Hello, Beth," I said. "I finally figured out why you looked so familiar to me. We were at the same luncheon about six months ago, weren't we B.C.?"

"Took you long enough, Custer!" the evil bearded publisher said as he entered the room through drapes behind the counter his wife leaned against. He was holding a dark Luger in his right hand.

"Hands in the air!" Watkins' voice bellowed from behind us, his M16 giving him an air of authority.

I wondered what happened to the real NSA guard assigned to watch Sundance.

Reluctantly, Zack, Buck, Sky and I lifted our hands and waited for J.C.'s other shoe to drop. It only took a couple of seconds.

"If it isn't the late Buck Jones," Carpenter said. "You haven't aged a bit in eighty years."

"Go fuck yourself!" Jones responded.

"Oh, I don't have to do that," the publisher responded. "I've got Beth for that."

The receptionist blushed and looked uncomfortable.

Then J.C. shocked all of us by saying, "And as if one cowboy hero isn't enough, we also have the late Steve McQueen!"

Even Lucky's jaw dropped at that one. Then two more armed thugs stepped into the lobby. One of them had a heavy pack on his back and a strange harpoon-like weapon in his hands. He snarled, pulled the trigger and a thick metal dart attached to a cable burst from the barrel and slammed into Lucky, causing a squealing noise that covered our friend's screams, as electrical arcs flashed all around him creating a powerful energy field. The crackling stopped and Lucky crumpled to the floor like an octopus dropped on a hot sidewalk.

"Oh, don't worry," Carpenter said. "He's not dead, yet."

"What did you do to him?" Sky adamantly asked.

"I just put him on ice for a while. Just consider that he's been shocked by an industrial-strength Taser."

"Why are you and your flunkies able to see him?" I asked.

"I gave the sight power to my assistants," J.C. admitted. "But as for me, your friend and I are distant relatives."

"Like the dragons," I said.

"Oh, you've met the dragons. I figured you had to have had some help in defeating our soldiers."

"So are you gonna take the professor's inventions and sell them?" Buck asked.

"Mr. Custer will tell you that I do like money," Carpenter said. "But this isn't about money. It's about time!"

"Speakin' of time," Prof. Ward Winston said as he entered the front door. "Let's get on with it!"

"Right you are, Winston old boy," J.C. said. "Watkins. You and Stanley drag our comatose cowboy to the elevator. Winston, you and Bridger cover Delaney and Blue. We'll need them downstairs."

The fake gate guard and the man with the backpack Taser struggled as they dragged our unconscious friend into the hall while the commie professor and the other thug herded Zack and Sky in the same direction. I was sure they were headed for the elevator. Carpenter nodded to his wife, who put a small whistle to her lips and blew. I couldn't hear anything, but maybe a couple of neighborhood German shepherds could.

The front door opened again and two more black-clad, armed thugs entered. They were wearing what looked like leather ski masks with matching headphones. Yep, I thought. Here come the dogs. The two toadies practically jumped to attention when they saw the publisher.

"Let's not leave a bloody mess in the lobby," J.C. said. "Take them to the conference room and kill them. Sorry Buck. But think of it this way. You started life more than one hundred and thirty years ago."

"Where do you want me, James?" Beth asked.

"Kill her too!" he ordered. "You're no longer necessary, Beth. You've served your purposes and now you will die."

"You bastard!" she screamed.

"Nobody's perfect," J.C. smiled and followed the gathering into the hall.

One of the masked men grabbed Beth by the arm and pushed her over next to Buck and me. "Get movin'!" They shoved their M16 barrels in our backs and pushed us down the hall toward the conference room. These two thugs were obviously experienced local killers, in that they were used to dealing with California victims—people who followed the strict gun laws and didn't carry concealed weapons. Unfortunately for them, Buck and I still had our pistols in the right pockets and our bayonets in the inside pockets of our jackets.

As we turned and led the way into the conference room, I shoved Beth against the first gunman to enter behind us. He stumbled backward as Beth fell to the floor, giving me a chance to whip my Colt .44 Magnum double-action revolver out of my pocket and blow a large hole through his leather-covered face. His partner dived over his body and rolled into a kneeling firing position with his M16. And he very easily could have blasted us all into eternity, if it hadn't been for quick-draw Buck, who fired three rounds into the dead center of his chest.

Beth was curled up on the floor sobbing as we confiscated the automatic rifles from the newly ventilated bodies. I grabbed the front of her blouse and yanked her toward me.

"What are they going to do with our friends?" I yelled in her face.

"They're all down on the time level," she stammered. "The elevator will be locked."

"And?" I said.

"And James and Winston have plans for the time portal," she continued. "They're going to gain access to several world leaders by going back to the past not more than an hour earlier so as not to cause that much damage to the time continuum."

She paused to catch her breath.

"They're going to assassinate presidents, premiers, prime ministers, chairmen and every other major government leader all at the same time, by going back and returning again and again until they are all dead. With Delaney's machine, they can do that one at a time and still have every official die at exactly the same moment. The world is going to be in complete panic. Violence will break out everywhere—pure chaos! That's J.C. and Winston's plan. With enough manipulation of recent history, they will completely destroy all of the civilizations of the world."

"And they think they'll end up running things?" I asked.

"J.C. is not a normal man. He has plans to rule the human rabble on all continents with an iron fist!"

I looked at Buck. "Zack will destroy the mechanism rather than allow those nuts access."

"No he won't," Beth said. "One of the research facilities James has acquired has developed drugs that can control minds. Zack and Sky will be put to use as zombies, as will others down the road."

"She's part of this," Buck said. "Let's kill her!"

"But you're a good guy," she spat. "You won't kill an unarmed woman."

"You're right, Beth," I explained. "But I'm not a 'good guy.' And I will kill you!"

I shoved the barrel of my new M16 against her belly, causing her to gasp, "No!"

"You believe the elevator will be locked at time level?" I asked.

"Yes."

"Is there any other way to get there?"

"When Prof. Delaney built this facility, he filled it with the most up-to-date, secure technology. But he also made sure to have some old-school backups. There's a hidden access port in his office."

"How does a receptionist know about such things?"

"I've seen the blueprints for this facility," she answered. "Prof. Delaney would be surprised at everything I've learned about Sundance Laboratories."

"Take us to the access port! And don't try anything or I'll blast your guts all over the walls!"

Buck put his hand on my shoulder. "Dave. If you're totin' one of the portable phones, you should probably call Agent Thorn. We might need some help on this."

"Yes, we could use some help. But we also don't want anyone to find out about the time travel mechanism. Once that cat's out of the bag, there'll be no way to put it back."

"But it's our government."

"Exactly," I said. "Would you like to see a gaggle of U.S. Congressmen and or generals deciding what to do with time-travel capabilities?"

"Point taken."

I yanked the former receptionist to her feet and shoved her into the hall. "Lead the way to Zack's office!"

"Your husband said he was a 'distant relative' of Lucky," Buck said. "What is he?"

"Up until a couple of years ago, I just thought he was a greedy, sociopathic, newspaper publisher."

"That was the general consensus," I added.

"Then he changed. It was like he became an evil puppet," she explained. "When he got excited about an acquisition, he almost glowed with a demonic energy."

I thought about that as we walked toward the office.

"Lucky told us there are all kinds of things that can travel through the time dimension," I said. "Some of those creatures are kind, he explained. But some are malevolent entities that leave a trail of destruction. He told us there are powerful things that can manipulate beings that may never even know of the evil creature's existence."

"Well, Beth," Buck stated. "I think we've identified your husband as basically the essence of evil. Now, how do we kill him?"

"If he can be killed," I added.

We entered Zack's amazing office. I say amazing because the wall was covered with classic movie posters from Saturday matinee serials, B-westerns and science fiction epics.

"Over here," Beth pointed at a very large framed poster from George Pal's 1960 production of H.G. Wells' "The Time Machine." In full color, the artwork depicted the beautiful Yvette Mimieux cowering behind Rod Taylor, who is holding a torch up to a monstrous Morlock. The film was a true classic of the sci-fi genre and the poster artwork was a masterpiece.

She reached up on the top of Zack's beautiful oak roll-top desk and pulled down one of the arms of an eight-inch statue of the Ray Harryhausen-animated beast from "20 Million Miles to Earth," causing "The Time Machine" poster to slide to the right, exposing a metal hatch. Beth spun the wheel in the center of the hatch, and pulled. It opened, revealing a vertical metal shaft that looked like it should hold a circular dumbwaiter elevator. Instead, it had a wall-mounted iron ladder that dropped straight down into the darkness.

"That's old school alright," I said. "Do we need miner helmets with lights on them?"

"As you reach each level, sensors will turn on lights to illuminate your descent," Beth stated.

"Good. Once again, you lead the way!"

The pretty brunette traitor climbed onto the ladder and began her downward progress. I slung my AR-15 on my shoulder and went next with Buck following me. Each time we reached a new level; small-embedded sconces brightened our way, as the prior level would go dark. Each level had a hatch entryway. At about sixty feet down, she announced we had arrived at the time level. Beth was first to step off the ladder onto a ledge, followed by me and then Buck. As quietly as possible I opened the hatch and we all entered a small room containing metal working equipment. There were grinders, lathes, drills and diamond-bladed saws. An impressive looking metal lathe caught my eye, mostly because of a small plate on it that identified it as having been manufactured by Acme Tools. I wondered if Wile E. Coyote had one of those. Then I mentally kicked myself for having such a stupid thought during a very serious situation. After all, what could a cartoon coyote do with a lathe?

"Now where?" Buck asked.

"We're on the other side of the ice chamber," Beth stated.

"Then we're going to have go through that door," I said. "And we have to do it very quietly. Beth. If you make the slightest noise, I will blow your head off!"

The woman looked at me with an expression of pure hate. But I figured she actually hated one person even more. The man she had lived with, served so faithfully and had become a traitor for, had ordered her death. I believed if she got the chance, she would make sure that J.C. had a "come to Jesus" moment, with her pulling the trigger.

I led the way as we crawled along behind the ice chamber. Buck kept a bayonet in his left hand, which also rested on Beth's shoulders. We could hear discussion coming from the other side of the amazing time machine. I quietly dragged myself forward on the glass floor to where I could see most of the control room through a grated cover on a switchbox. Zack was seated in a chair behind a short table where his laptop sat open in front of him. Just to his left, Sky also sat quietly in a chair. Both of them were staring straight ahead with blank expressions on their faces. Next to them was a medical over-bed table on rollers, on which I could see a folded white towel containing a hypodermic syringe and a small bottle.

Shit! I thought. They've been drugged.

Bridger stood near the entry to the lab with his M16 at port arms, while Watkins stayed directly behind the professor and Sky with his rifle pointed at the floor and his eyes lustfully washing over the beautiful blonde. Lucky was lying on his back on the round slab within the glass oval where I first saw the cloned body of Buck Jones. Standing near where the small gun-barrel-like projections pointed down toward our unconscious Steve McQueen-looking pal Stanley, who was still wearing his backpack Taser gun, Winston and a smiling J.C. preparing for the most destructive assault on civilizations ever perpetrated. The green glow that emanated from below the glass floor caused J.C. to look appropriately cadaverous.

"You may still be physically paralyzed," the evil publisher ranted at Lucky. "But I know you can hear me. And because we are related species, although I am far superior, I know I cannot kill you—just as no one will ever be able to kill me. So, thanks to Prof. Delaney, I'm going to do the next best thing and send you on a little trip back in time to the original Jurassic park, some two-hundred-million years in the past. Perhaps you'll find out that some dinosaurs may actually enjoy country-western music."

Stanley started to back away from the table as J.C. said, "Prof. Delaney. Are we targeted for two-hundred-million years ago?"

In a drone-like voice that would have made a Gregorian chant sound like scat singing, Zack answered, "Yes sir. Ready to go."

"Then start your engine!" J.C. ordered.

The ice chamber apparatus began to rumble and, once again, I knew time was running out. As Stanley turned to move back farther into the laboratory and away from the glass oval, I leaped up and shoved my bayonet into his throat. Buck fired two shot from his M16. One splattered Watkins' brain onto the wall and one nearly beheaded Bridger. J.C. turned angrily to face me while I held Stanley's gurgling body to my front.

"It's too late to save your friend!" J.C. yelled.

I answered my former boss by reaching around his dying minion, pointing the backpack Taser at him and pulling the trigger. A thick metal dart attached to a cable struck the evil man in the chest, accompanied by glowing electrical energy arcing off his body and illuminating a translucent completely alien shape. The energy beast writhed in pain, its ape-like arms reaching up and clawing at the lightning shooting off its form. Three large red eyes burned angrily in my direction while the beast that was a third-rate weekly publisher roared and every nerve in its evil body must have felt like it was on fire.

"Turn it off, Zack!" I yelled.

Then I heard Steve McQueen's voice yell, "Don't stop, Zack! Send us back!"

"...SEND YOU ON A LITTLE TRIP..."

The 50s television cowboy's arms reached around the struggling beast, pulling it onto the round table. "Now! Pull the switch, Igor!"

I dropped Stanley's corpse at the same time that the blinding light flashed in the room and the mechanism screamed like an eighteen-wheeler sliding sideways on the 405 Freeway during rush hour. The noise and light died instantly, leaving a dim, eerie silence and an empty circular table.

"They're gone!" I said.

"Lucky sacrificed himself for civilization!" Buck exclaimed. "Talk about a real hero!"

Prof. Ward Winston was curled up on the floor rubbing his eyes. Beth stood wide-eyed and stoop-shouldered between Buck and me while glaring at where her husband had vanished. Zack and Sky continued to sit in their chairs, quietly staring straight ahead. And although my mind was digesting just how important it was that we had succeeded in heading off this possible worldwide disaster, I just felt so empty as I tallied the cost.

I slowly walked up to Winston and looked down at him. He pulled his hands away from his eyes and looked back up at me with a sneer of disdain. That's when I kicked him in the face.

"Buck. Make sure he doesn't have any weapons. Then, if he moves, kick him again."

"With pleasure," the big cowboy said, while keeping a good grip on Beth's left arm.

"Zack! Sky! Can you hear me?"

They both answered, "Yes," as they continued looking somewhere beyond my vision.

"Do you know where you are?"

"Yes," Zack answered. "What would you like us to do?"

"Stay put!" I said. "Beth! Get over here!"

Buck shoved her in my direction.

"Have you ever seen your husband use this drug before?"

"Uh-huh," she answered as if she no longer cared about anything. "He experimented on some of Winston's students."

"Does the drug wear off?"

"It may take up to a day," she said. "But, yes."

I pulled a chair away from the wall and told the former receptionist to, "Sit down!"

Then I filled the hypodermic with about a quarter inch of the chemical that was shot into Zack and Sky and I shoved the needle into her shoulder just below her neck. She moaned, dropped her head forward and, while I held on to her arm, sat straight back up with a dead expression on her formerly pretty face.

"You are a traitor to your country and I should kill you!" I said.

"Yes. I am. And you should."

"Are you ready to do what you are told?" I asked.

"Yes. I am."

"Good. Stay seated. Buck. Help me put these three bodies on the round table."

Buck smiled as he began to understand my plan. We dragged the corpses of Watkins, Stanley and Bridger into the glass oval and plopped them on the circular timetable.

I said to Buck, "Now let's go upstairs and bring down those other chunks of ski-mask-wearing meat and add them to the pile." I paused. Then I added, "Zack. You and Sky just stay here. We'll be right back."

"Yes sir."

"Beth. You're coming with us."

"Yes sir."

I began to feel like a rear-echelon cherry lieutenant with all the yes sirs.

"What about Prof. Shit For Brains?" Buck asked.

"We're gonna want to ask him some questions later," I said. "Is there any way you can make sure he doesn't cause any trouble for a couple of hours?"

The crack of Buck's rifle butt against the Berkeley professor's skull echoed throughout the laboratory.

"Works for me," I said. "Let's go."

I put Beth to work with a mop and a bucket cleaning up the messes that the two dead dog-whistle boys made, while Buck and I took the bodies down to the time level and stacked them on top of their comrades. Perhaps, I thought, I'm helping the former receptionist learn a new trade. Then I shook my head, knowing that J.C.'s widow was not going to be released back into the wild.

"Now comes the fun part of my plan," I said.

"I think I know what that is," Buck smiled.

"Zack. You still awake?"

"Yes sir."

"Can you set the target time to be within the same million years or so as the last one?" I asked. "You know, still in the early Jurassic Period?"

"Yes sir."

"Then let's just shoot this pile of vermin back to that time, somewhere in a steamy jungle."

"Yes sir."

The mechanism rumbled, screamed and the bright light flashed. Then it became very quiet again, and the table was bare.

"It had to have been quite a feeding time in the world's very first wild animal refuge," I said.

"Waste not, want not," Buck added.

"Now let's get Zack and Sky up to the hospital room where they can sleep off the drug," I said. "And we need to take the commie professor with us."

Buck tossed Winston over his shoulder in a fireman's carry while I gently herded Sky and Zack into the elevator. The two amazing scientists had the same expression on their faces, showing all the emotion of Ed Sullivan and Al Gore riding in an elevator. When we got to the hospital room, I took the scientists to the two beds and gave them orders.

"Lie down. Put your heads on the pillows. Get some sleep."

"Yes sir," they both said.

Then I sent Beth back down to the time level. "There are a few bloody drag trails on the floor for you to mop up and some splatter on the walls that you should clean off."

"Yes sir."

"As soon as you are through, put the mop, bucket and supplies where they belong and come to the conference room."

"Yes sir."

I asked Buck to tie and gag the traitorous college professor in "one of those cushy high-backed chairs" in the conference room, while I made sure that Zack and Sky were comfortable. Both of them were sound asleep. I knew I would have to contact Agent Thorn pretty soon, if only to report the lack of a guard in the parking lot. But there were still a few hot irons that needed to cool down.

Winston and Beth both had to be dealt with one way or another. And I was definitely going to take the time to thoroughly interrogate the Berkeley commie before I tied up that loose end. I knew that if I turned over the traitorous former receptionist and the half-dead revolutionary leader of the People's Brigade to the feds, a gaggle of corrupt politicians and prosecutors, and their media buddies, would descend on Sundance Labs, and me personally, for having taken the alleged law into our own hands.

The government would take full possession of Sundance Laboratory's scientific achievements while creating its own fake news narrative regarding the situation. Zack and Sky would probably be placed in a black-site laboratory in the middle of nowhere to live their lives out as political prisoners, while being ordered to work on weaponizing time travel, tissue cloning, and anything else their chemical interrogations brought to the NSA's attention.

My brain showed me visuals of classic western star Buck Jones being strapped to a table in some secret Area 51 "hangar" laboratory next to a spindly gray alien being, while some former German scientist was vivisecting them both alive. I realized that I was allowing my imagination to run wild with B-film-reference fantasies, again, but they weren't that far from the possible truth.

I also knew that once the spooks finished interrogating me about our efforts, I wouldn't be of much use. After all, the government had enough puff-piece writers on the payroll, including *The New York Times*, *The Washington Post* and most of the television network "journalists." I pictured my beaten, battered body being marched out into the Nevada desert, pushed to my knees and a Luger held to the back of my head. When the mental fantasy cut to a close up an evilly grinning Conrad Veidt pulling the trigger and laughing, I shook my head and said, "Enough!"

"Enough is right!" Beth's angry voice brought my thoughts back to reality.

Buck walked into the hospital room with his hands in the air. Beth was right behind him, an M16 gripped tightly in her hands.

"Did you finish cleaning up the time level?" I asked.

"Very funny, dead man," she spat. "I see your friends are still under the influence. What I didn't tell you downstairs is that my husband had also experimented with the zombie formula on me. And although it worked for a while, I have built up a resistance to that chemical, which allowed me to shake off its effects rather quickly."

"Well, I must say, Beth," I stalled. "If you didn't completely clean that spattered wall in the time lab, I'm going to have to write up a demerit for you on this month's job performance."

The once beautiful former receptionist looked like she had been sparring with Rocky Balboa in that butcher-shop meat locker. Her hair was twisted and hanging down on her shoulders, while her hands, arms and dress were covered with splotches of blood. The insanity of a very lost woman sparkled from her darting eyes. If I didn't figure out something quickly, we would all soon be dead.

She lifted the rifle to point directly at me as she said, "You'll die first, Custer!"

The shot was loud as I stepped back and looked down at my chest. She missed, I thought. Then both Buck and I saw the small red dot in Beth's solar plexus expand as blood rapidly saturated the front of her dress. Her knees buckled and she dropped to the floor face first. I quickly snatched up her M16.

"What? How?" Buck asked.

Then we heard the amazing voice of Jimmie Rodgers sing, "I had a friend named Ramblin' Bob, who used to steal, gamble and rob. He thought he was the smartest guy in town."

The singing brakeman walked in strumming his guitar and continuing to sing "In the Jailhouse Now," as he stepped over Beth. Throwing his head back, he grinned and yodeled while Buck and I stood flatfooted with our mouths open and question marks in our eyes.

My brain searched for the right words and came up with, "What the hell, Lucky?"

"You boys didn't think I was gonna stay back there with a bunch of dinosaur music haters, did you?"

He reached into his pocket and pulled a metal tag like the one Zack clipped on my shirt when I headed back to 1942.

"I understand Zack's been lookin' for this," he said. "I took it off you, knowing I might need a return ticket at some time."

I laughed and slapped him on the back. "You're a smart cookie, Lucky."

"And don't you forget it, pal."

"Just what was it like back in the Jurassic days?"

"Well," he said. "I was only there for a few seconds. But it was hot, sticky and your former publisher was still sound asleep."

"Anything else you can remember?" Buck asked.

"I looked around and didn't see Jeff Goldblum, so I left."

Buck didn't quite understand, but I got a laugh out of the smartass wraith as he then reached into his pocket and handed me a revolver.

"I picked that up on the way to save your ass," he said. "Poor, sweet Beth just wasn't that nice of a woman after all."

I looked down at the receptionist's body and mumbled, "Now who the hell is gonna clean that up?"

"It looks like Zack and Sky are going to be asleep for a while," Buck said. "The commie professor is strapped up good and tight in the conference room. And all three of us have been a smidge busy. Let's grab a beer."

First we dragged the former receptionist's body out of the hospital room and into the broom closet. Then we went to the break room and opened the small refrigerator, which contained exactly three cold bottles of Miller High Life.

"Perfect," I said, as I handed out the other two. Holding up my bottle I said, "Here's to the return of our old friend Jimmie Rodgers."

We all took a drink and then Lucky began to yodel again.

"Save it for when Zack and Sky recover," I said, hoping not to hurt the goofball's feelings. "So what do you guys want to do next?"

"There are no more beers in that fridge, so that's out," Buck said. "Perhaps we should just go get Winston's interview done."

"That's a fine choice," I said.

Jimmie Rodgers then adopted a Stan Laurel expression and said, "It certainly is."

I looked at him and shook my head. We knew we had to forgive the singing wraith's quirky behavior, especially since he had not only saved our lives several times, but all of the world's civilizations as well.

The commie professor was awake and not very happy when we arrived at the conference room. I reached over and yanked the gag off and out of his mouth. He spat and started cursing.

"I'll see all of you murdering fascists behind bars!" he yelled. "I have my rights! My attorneys will crucify you!"

Buck looked at me and asked, "Should we just kill him now and be done with it?"

"That's tempting," I said. "But I think we otta give him a chance to confess his sins."

"I've faced down fascist Fox News reporters," Winston said. "I can handle a two-bit fluff writer and a hillbilly!"

I smiled and gave him a first-rate Moe Howard two-fingertips-in-the-eyes poke. He shook his head, tears ran out of his eyes and he said some not-so-nice things to me.

Buck looked at me with an odd expression while I explained, "I just always wanted to do that."

"I know what you're thinking," Lucky said. "You can beat the information out of him. But, why go through all that when we can simply place him in front of a white background that couldn't be traced and videotape him while he admits to his traitorous behavior and also lists off the names of people he has bribed, enemies who have bribed him and all of his socialist henchmen."

"Yeah," Winston snarled. "Good luck with that, assholes!"

"Dave," Lucky said. "Do you remember how I made you sing 'Cow Cow Boogie'?"

I felt my face flush and I answered through clenched teeth. "Yes!"

"I can do the same for the Judas professor," Jimmie Rodgers explained.

"I think anyone watching the video might have questions if his mouth was being opened and closed without his lips syncing up to his voice."

"I have another way of doing that, Dave. I didn't do it with you because, well, that would be wrong. But with this guy, what've we got to lose?"

I knew Winston, like the late Watkins, Stanley and Bridger, had been anointed by J.C. earlier in the evening to be able to see entities like Lucky. So I wasn't surprised to catch a flicker of fear cross his face as he listened to our time-traveling minstrel.

"I'm interested in seeing what you're describing," I said. "Let's find a blank wall and shove this bum up against it. I'll see if I can round up a decent video camera."

Buck and Lucky dragged the bound professor and his high-backed chair up against a white wall at the far end of the conference room. I walked back toward Zack's office, but decided to check in on Zack and Sky on the way. When I opened the hospital room door I saw Zack sitting up on the edge of his bed. He looked up at me and asked, "Did we lose anybody other than Lucky?"

"Welcome back, boss," I said. "Buck and I are just fine. And the real good news is, Lucky made it back."

"How'd he do that? I remember being a drugged-up robot following orders to send him to prehistoric times."

"Do you also remember looking for one of the small metal tabs that I took back to 1942? You know, my return ticket?"

"You mean Lucky had it?"

I nodded and the scientist laughed. "That boy is one tricky devil. Thank God for that!"

"Hey, Custer!" Sky's head turned on her pillow. "I'm here as well."

I rushed over and embraced her, then quickly stepped back worried that I might hurt her. "How do you feel?"

"Like I'm no longer a zombie," she said with a smile. "And I could use a beer."

I looked at my watch and saw it was past midnight. "Both of you could also use some more sleep. That was a pretty strong drug that they shot into you."

"I'll sleep tomorrow," Zack said. "Right now I'd like to know what took place after you put us up here. And I'd like to see Buck and Lucky."

"Yeah," Sky added. "Me too."

"Why don't you two take your time getting on your feet, go use the restroom and then join us in the conference room," I said. "Oh, and Zack. Do you have a good video camera?"

"Can't you use a cellphone?" he asked.

"I'd like something with a little better quality for Prof. Ward Winston's confession," I explained. "We need to either make DVDs for mail delivery or find an untraceable way to send the videos through the Internet to all major news agencies as well as city, state and federal law enforcement."

"Damn, son," Zack said. "You have been busy. I do have a way to deliver your exposé via the Internet, and no agency will be able to trace it back to us."

"I've got a good camera in the lockers," Sky said. "I'll bring it with me when I join you."

I returned to the conference room where the terrified commie was tied to a chair up against the wall. His gag had been strapped back on him, according to Lucky, to keep Buck from punching his lights out. I gave my friends the good news about Zack and Sky's recovery and that a video camera was on the way.

"So you think you can really make him tell the truth?" I asked Jimmie Rodgers.

"Yeah," Buck added. "The truth is an alien concept to pieces of shit like him."

"Not gonna be a problem, boys. Just watch. Once you get the camera set up, I'll explain as I go."

Refreshed and smiling, the blonde beauty and the research scientist stepped into the room and into a series of hugs and greetings. Sky brought the camera and its stand and Zack carried a six-pack of Miller High Life.

"Where'd you find the brews?" Buck asked. "We cleaned out the ones in the break room."

"I have several beer fridges in this facility," Zack answered. "We may be all about amazing scientific research, but we also take care of our common-sense needs."

Five happy people drank, laughed and commented on how glad they were to see each other while one man sat and scowled at the gathering.

"By the way," Sky said. "Someone has a job to take care of later, in that Beth is leaking into the hallway under the broom closet door."

"You just can't find good help these days," I said. Then I turned and looked at Winston. "And there might be more leaking before we're done."

I set up the video camera on its tripod facing the traitor.

"Are you ready for your close-up, Mr. Winston?"

He glared into the lens while I made sure no ropes were visible in the video frame.

"Okay, Lucky. How're you going to do this?"

"Watch this, kids," he said. "You're gonna love it."

Jimmie Rodgers stepped in front of the man and ripped off his gag. Then, while Winston's eyes grew larger, Lucky transformed into a huge boa constrictor and began wrapping himself around the tied-up Marxist maniac. With his red forked tongue moving in and out of his mouth, Lucky's devilish reptilian head lowered itself to be eyeball to eyeball with his strangling victim. The snake's muscles rippled under its scaly skin as it tightened, causing Winston to turn red and gasp for air.

The constrictor's jaw dropped, opening its mouth wide as if to swallow the man. Then, with a final surge of strength, it squeezed and lights flashed as it vanished inside Prof. Ward Winston, who took a deep breath and looked up at us.

The commie bastard closed his eyes, opened his mouth and began to yodel.

"What the hell?" I said.

"Hi guys," he said, in Jimmie Rodgers' voice. "It's me. I'm in here."

We all looked at each other.

"I repeat," I said. "What the hell?"

"Well, duh. I'm Lucky. I'm inside this very disgusting man. I have access to his knowledge, memory and deepest thoughts. And hold on to your hats boys and girls. If you thought J.C. was an evil son of bitch, you haven't been in here. Holy Caligula! This guy is a piece of work. Mix Khrushchev, Mao, Castro, Hitler and Pol Pot and you'd have a kitten compared to wacky Ward Winston."

"So what's the plan?"

"You're gonna tape me, as Prof. Ward Winston, admitting to a variety of his real traitorous criminal acts."

"You might want to change your voice to sound like him instead of an early 20th Century country singer," I suggested.

"Oh, yeah," he said in Winston's voice.

I turned on the video camera, smiled and said, "Action!" And the big ham started his monologue.

"I am Prof. Ward Winston of the University of California, Berkeley," he said with a straight face. "And I am a communist. I have been teaching young minds to share my beliefs and your wealth, and have paid many young people to lead protests into violence as an act of revolution. For several years I have accepted money from Communist China, a variety of former Soviet governments, Cuba and other enemy nations to subvert the American way of life. Some large multi-national corporations fronting for those same governments have been very supportive of my efforts to destroy capitalism, democracy and individual rights through attempts to bring about chaos."

We watched silently as Lucky admitted to every act of corruption, bribery, sabotage, arson, murder, terrorism and torture that Winston had been involved with in any way. He listed off the names of all enemy agents who paid him or dealt with him in and out of the country. The names of the leaders of the People's Brigade red mercenaries were revealed, as well as their acts of planned revolution disguised as anti-fascist protests.

I was sure, once the feds saw the tape, they would be very busy rounding up corporate spies, anti-American business interests, and celebrities, elected officials and government employees who were actually on the take from people like Winston and his handlers.

Something that might unite even the most liberal of Americans, maybe even Hollywood celebrities, against the enemy was when Winston completely destroyed his façade as an extreme leftist social warrior by his admission of a variety of fundraising measures, such as drug sales and human trafficking. His sponsor governments sent thousands of sex slaves into America to serve the lowest forms of life in the country through prostitution, pornography and blackmail entrapment of several named members of Congress, including at least one on the House Intelligence Committee. Having been a big wheel in the human-trafficking pipeline, Winston garnered millions of dollars to continue his violent efforts toward chaos. He also admitted to having herded some of his college students into prostitution and drug manufacturing and sales.

Lucky, fully aware of Winston's innermost desires, confessed to some of the most vile behavior a human being could ever become involved in before concluding his distasteful diatribe about himself.

"I am admitting all of this under my own free will. I have achieved my many successes because I hate America! I hate Americans! And now that my efforts to destroy this country are being exposed, I have shared the wealth of my pain with all of you who were foolish enough to join me in my quest, whether you were doing it because of political beliefs, need for power or just greed. I hate all of you too!

"Copies of these remarks will be sent to law enforcement and all print and broadcast news agencies in America, as well as some in Canada, Mexico and the United Kingdom. I'm leaving now, and I'm pretty sure no one will be able to find me."

Fade to black.

With a gasp of air, Winston slumped forward as far as his ropes allowed. Lucky, as Jimmie Rodgers, appeared standing next to me. He shuddered and said, "Bleaughidda," as if trying to get a very bad taste out of his mouth.

I palmed Winston on the forehead to get him to look up into my eyes.

"You were a very talkative piece of shit," I said. "Now that you've turned over a new leaf and told some truth, would you like us to drop you somewhere? How about Chinatown? I'm not sure, but as soon as your speech hits the Internet, I'll bet there may be some mainland-supporting Tongs that will want to have a conversation with you; maybe cut to the chase. And then again, perhaps they might decide to send you to Beijing. I hear it's always harvest season over there, and your organs have to be worth something."

"If we let him loose, that would be just as bad as killing him where he sits," Sky said.

"But nowhere near as much fun," Buck stated.

"It's too bad we're not up in the Hualapai Mountains," she continued. "I'll bet some of our tribal warrior friends would take him off our hands."

"Hey," Lucky said. "Don't worry about it. I got this covered. Get him on his feet and let's go out to the lobby."

We all looked at each other and, considering everything Lucky had done for us so far, we did what he asked. We left Winston's hands tied behind him, but untied his feet and walked him to the lobby.

"Now, if someone would just open the front door, we'll be fine," he requested.

I held the door wide and, in a flash of light, a giant invisible dragon grabbed Prof. Ward Winston in its talons and flashed out the door and into the early morning sky like a rocket.

"You gotta admit it," I said. "That boy is talented."

"Let's go have another beer," Sky said, while taking my hand and smiling.

CHAPTER THIRTEEN
BANSHEES AND BLESSINGS

While we sipped our beers and truly relaxed for the first time in a while, my thoughts returned to the facility security, specifically, what happened to the NSA guard that Watkins pretended to be? It was almost sunrise when Buck and I decided to do a quick recon of the brushy area around the parking lot.

"We don't know if Watkins killed the real guard, had him kidnapped or just put him to sleep for a while," I said. "But if he's out here, we need to find him."

"Sure thing, Dave. I'm also watchin' for tracks, blood spatter or anything that might tell us what may have happened."

We started at the pull-in area to the parking lot and continued to inspect the complete perimeter of the property. There wasn't a trace of evidence that a killing, kidnapping or anything else took place. We couldn't even find a federal vehicle parked in the area that an agent might have used to get to his post.

"It looks like the guard just vanished," Buck said. "This really complicates things."

"Yeah. The thug who pretended to be an NSA agent is long gone. And Agent Thorn is going to have some questions regarding this situation for sure."

We reported our concerns to Zack, who said he would contact Agent Thorn and "play it by ear."

We spent the next several hours winding down from our adventures. Zack used his super secret computer skills to send off the infamous Ward Winston confession to all pertinent agencies and websites.

Meanwhile, Buck cleaned up the broom closet and hallway spill, while Sky took inventory of the facility. Beth was given a makeshift burial in the South China Sea two weeks into the future to avoid any compromise of the time continuum. I'd like to say that she wore a delightfully glittering Gucci strapless gown with the latest colorful social-awareness ribbon for her final farewell to our world, but that would be a lie. We wrapped her in cheap-black, plastic trash bags that could easily be breached by the sharp-toothed denizens of the deep.

Between naps, exercise, meals, beers and planning sessions, we kept apprised of the world's reaction to the video. A variety of news accounts concerning the Berkeley commie's confession appeared on news broadcasts and in print publications. Social media gurus erased all tweets, posts and shares concerning the video and its allegations. Local, state and federal law enforcement raided a plethora of alleged enemy compounds and were caught on camera herding arrested individuals into large windowless vans for transport to lockups.

The *New York Post* called the situation an act of war, while some CNN pontificators continued to refer to the video as misinformation manufactured by Russian assets. UC Berkeley administrators put out a press release, with no attribution, denying any knowledge of Prof. Winston's non-university activities. That educational institution also created several new "safe spaces" on campus that didn't allow any newspapers, news broadcasts or T-shirts that referred to Winston or his confession. A large number of students gathered in those spaces to hold what some radio and television talk-show hosts referred to as a "massive left-coast cry-in." *The Washington Post* demanded transparency from the federal government concerning the ongoing raids while Sean Hannity called for Congress to investigate all allegations of communist infiltration in the U.S. government. Congress was too confused to act, in that several representatives and senators had mysteriously disappeared and leadership of those institutions were being challenged from within.

Numerous activist organizations, including members of the "anti-fascist" People's Brigade, launched violent riots in Los Angeles, Chicago and Portland, only to be put down quickly when the president sent members of the 101st Airborne Division in to deal with them. The troopers were successful in saving a lot of small businesses from destruction and, at the same time, capturing many Brigade revolutionaries. The ACLU was outraged.

In response to one of the most asked questions nationally, a children's book publisher, in a smart entrepreneurial move, instantly released a large hardback publication of cartoons containing at least a hundred silly characters on each page. The "Where's Prof. Ward Winston?" book was originally set to be published with another well-known character, but he was removed and replaced by a funny caricature of the commie professor wearing a striped shirt and knit cap. The country's remaining bookstores and Amazon warehouses couldn't keep up with the demand for copies.

I was relaxing in my La-Z-Boy recliner at my Redondo Beach bungalow while sipping a Lucky Lager and listening to the news on my Crosley radio when an anchorman played several sound bites from Hollywood celebrities concerning recent headlines. One elderly washed-up actor, who had spent his life portraying the same gangster character over and over, claimed he wanted to punch whoever faked the confession video in the nose. Another male action star, whose films had been boycotted for the prior six years, said America should enforce a new "bamboo curtain" of sanctions against Red China. I turned off the radio when I heard a former first lady call the situation a "right-wing conspiracy."

"So what else is new?" Jimmie Rodgers said, as he walked out of my kitchen with a can of beer in his hand.

"Hey! You're back! How was your flight?"

"Can't complain. They didn't serve peanuts."

"Is everything going well for the tribal warriors?"

"Oh, I didn't go to Arizona," Lucky said. "I was up in the Cascade Mountains in northern California."

That surprised me. "What's up there other than pot gardens and out of work lumberjacks?"

"You know, while I was rooting around in Winston's brain, I discovered he was involved in what he called an 'environmentalist movement.' He and his co-conspirators were working to 'save the environment' by shutting down industry and energy concerns in western governments. Of course, he was fully aware and supportive of the black-sky smokestack industries that spewed poison into the air in his favorite dictatorships."

"Par for the course."

"So I got the idea that perhaps he could use a little true environmental education," he explained. "And I have these friends up north who were glad to mentor the man."

"That's certainly nice of them," I said. "Do you think he'll learn anything?"

"He doesn't have a choice in the matter. They put him on as an intern."

"Who are these folks? Are they native Americans?"

"Yes, in a way," he said. "I've known them for many years. They're mostly peaceful and extremely large. They live in an area I like to call Sasquatch Mountain."

"You left him with Bigfoots?"

"Gee, Dave. Wouldn't that be Bigfeet?"

And with that I felt like life had returned to my *new* normal.

•••

Earlier that day, I had dropped off Sammy's Christmas presents at my sister's house. And, having considered Linda my very best friend for most of my life (except for that time she destroyed my Sarah Michelle Gellar "Buffy" poster), I decided to tell her about my new job and some of the activities I had been part of recently. Fortunately, I had arrived at breakfast time, so even if she called the cops and had me sent to the Hawthorne Ha-Ha Asylum For the Terminally Nuts, I'd get some bacon and eggs.

"Hey, Uncle Dave!" Sammy hollered as he ran into the kitchen and jumped on my lap.

"How're you, big fella?"

"Swell! When are we gonna go see Betty Boop again?"

"Soon. But, you know, there are more important things to do tomorrow."

"You bet! It's Christmas!"

"That's right," Linda said. "And Uncle Dave brought you some gifts that I just put under the tree."

Sammy jumped to the floor and ran into the living room to see if he could figure out what was inside the wrapped boxes. I was smart enough to make sure the presents wouldn't rattle when he shook them.

Linda leaned down and whispered in my ear. "You didn't get him another belt-set of cap guns, did you? There are some neighborhood moms who would call for the SWAT team if they saw him wearing one of those, again."

"No, Linda," I said defensively. "But I did get a great deal on a mint GI Joe with his own tank. Sammy's gonna love it!"

She rolled her eyes and poured me some coffee.

"I've got a new job," I said, as I plucked a couple of strips of bacon off a plate and spread some marmalade on my toast.

"I thought somethin' was up, since I hadn't heard from you for a couple of days. I'll bet they'll certainly miss you at the *Banner*."

"Yep," I said. "I don't think they'll be able to continue without me."

Once she and Sammy sat down at the breakfast table, I started in on my tale.

"I now work for a scientific think tank," I said. "And I recently traveled through time to 1942 and returned with Buck Jones."

Linda's stoic expression didn't change as, I'm sure, she was wondering how she was going to get all of the butter knives out of my reach. Sammy grinned and said, "You mean Buck from the Rough Riders?"

"That's right, Sammy. And, together, we fought off commie spies while dealing with dragons, a banshee and tribal ghosts."

"Wow!" my nephew exclaimed, while his mother slowly pushed herself away from the table.

"Really, Linda. Hear me out."

She exhaled and pulled herself and her chair back to hear my ramblings.

Then I started from the beginning, when I went for the interview at Sundance Laboratories. Because of Sammy, I kept the violence down in my descriptions of various altercations. But even my cleaned up version of things

"YOU DIDN'T GET HIM...CAP-GUNS, DID YOU?"

took more than an hour. When I was done, right after explaining how Lucky had turned into an invisible dragon and flown the traitorous professor out the door, I took my last sip of cold coffee and waited.

Sammy had a million questions, while Linda just stared at me for a while. Then she asked me if I had eaten any suspicious brownies or fallen asleep in a recently painted room.

"How does Lucky change from one singer to another?" my nephew asked.

"I don't know."

"If you went back in time and met yourself, would you melt like in 'Time Cop'?"

"That's a good one. I hope I don't find out."

"What does invisible dragon poop look like?"

"Dragons are kind of shy. I didn't see any of them pooping."

"Is the banshee married?"

"Wow! Maybe she was and now she's just a typical ex-wife."

"When do I get to meet Bob the biting Morgan?"

"Perhaps we'll all go to the Wailing Banshee Ranch in the spring and you can meet Bob."

"Is Sky as pretty as you describe her?"

"She's even prettier."

Linda shook her head and said, "Brother. I think it's time I stopped worrying about you. Whatever you've done, I want you to know we're here to support you, no matter what."

"Does that mean I'm still invited for Christmas dinner?"

"Of course."

"Can I bring my friends Zack, Buck, Sky and, if he's in town, Lucky?"

"Say yes, Mom!"

"Of course, but you'll have to bring dessert."

"Great. I'll bring three apple pies and two cases of Miller High Life."

"Your friends drink a lot?"

"No more than me."

"Better bring three cases," my smartass sister said.

●●●

I drove to Sundance Laboratories with Lucky to let everyone know about our invite to Christmas dinner. We met in the conference room where Lucky brought everyone up to speed on his trip to the Cascades. I sipped my beer and calmly listened while everyone else threw a million questions at the wraith concerning Sasquatch Mountain. I relaxed while thinking that I had finally progressed to a spot where nothing seemed to surprise me. Time travel? Yep. Spirits? Sure. Dragons? You betchum. Banshees? Yes sir. Bigfoot? Well, duh.

"On a positive note," Zack said. "Thanks to the professor's amazing confession, a big dent is being pounded into the violent rebellion movement that's been destroying a lot of businesses and lives in this country. Foreign spies, handlers, moles, blackmailers and homegrown traitors are being rounded up and branded as the destructive critters they are. Winston's words were like the beginning of a long tumbling domino effect, taking down a deadly enemy before an actual war could begin.

"On the other hand," he continued, "we have some collateral damage to deal with because of Agent Thorn's missing guard. In about an hour, Thorn is going to come by to discuss the situation. Let's just bring him into this room and quietly listen to what he has to say. He may not be able to spend much time on a missing agent problem in that, with all the roundups going on, he has a lot of hot situations to deal with."

There was a pause in the discussion, and I took advantage of the lull to announce the real important news. "I just want to let everyone know that you are all invited to Christmas dinner tomorrow at my sister's house," I said. "And I really hope you all can come."

"Well, Dave," Buck said. "I don't know. I'm supposed to have dinner at Yak Canutt's place, and... Oh, yeah. It's not 1942. Sure. I'll be there."

"That sounds great!" Sky said. "I'd love to."

"I really appreciate that, Dave," Zack stated. "Us lonely absent-minded professors never turn down a dinner invite."

"Will you have live music?" Lucky asked.

"Only if you're there," I answered.

"Then it's a done deal."

Zack's phone dinged and he took a quick look at the screen. "It's Thorn. He and two other agents are early. They're at the door now. Let's go let them in. And Lucky, just keep as quiet as possible."

"No problem, boss. I'll just be a fly on the wall, minus the buzz."

Zack opened the door and the three men entered the lobby.

"I'll bet you're a fairly busy man these days, Agent Thorn," Zack said, while shaking hands with the fed.

"Things are jumping," Thorn said. "Professor, this is Agent Curruthers and Agent Sane."

The two blue-suited feds nodded in our direction.

"Have you folks been watching the news?" Thorn asked.

"We've kept an eye on the headlines," Zack said. "I'd say your agency is gonna pay out a sizeable chunk of overtime during the next several months."

"I believe there'll be an emergency increase in our budget. I just wish I could get my hands on Winston. He's the prize with our game."

"Good luck," Zack said. "What can we do for you?"

"You know we're looking for our missing agent," Thorn stated. "And we were wondering if there is any way he may have gotten into your building."

"I don't know how he could have done that," Zack responded.

"Agent Watkins and I had traded shifts in your parking lot for a few days," Curruthers said. "And then he vanished."

I felt a sharp nudge in my calm demeanor as I glanced at Buck, who started backing toward the hall.

"Did Agent Watkins have a scar on his chin?" Sky asked.

"Yes he did," Thorn said. "But, how did you know?"

"Curruthers, you idiot!" Sane yelled, as he whipped a 9mm Glock out from under his jacket. "They're onto us!"

"What are you doing?" Thorn hollered. "Put that away!"

Curruthers joined Sane in covering us with his weapon.

"Get your hands up, Thorn!" Sane ordered. "Everybody, stay frozen! You move. You die!"

"What the hell?" Thorn sputtered.

"It looks like the commies have infiltrated your agency too," I said.

"Shut up, Custer!" Curruthers said. "Where are Watkins, Winston and the others?"

"Maybe all of your friends went on the lam with blabbermouth Winston," I stalled. "You know you men are in deep trouble. Hanoi Jane may have gotten off, but I think you traitors will probably be shot."

I really felt naked in that none of us had any of our weapons with us. I could see our invisible Josh Randall "fly on the wall" standing not too far from Curruthers. I slightly shook my head back and forth in Lucky's direction to let him know not to make a play, yet. If he dropped the one agent, Sane could get a shot off and I didn't want any bloodshed, on our side anyway.

I figured those two assholes were panic-stricken that their traitorous comrades had vanished, leaving them with no organization, no payoffs and no hope of escaping justice. They apparently knew the Sundance facility was a priority target for Winston and his handler. And, I'm sure, they figured out that some sort of attempt was made to raid the labs by the Berkeley bastard, Watkins and others from their side.

"We want what Winston wanted!" Curruthers said.

"And what's that?" I was pushing it. "Money? Your own reality show? A timeshare condo in Fort Lauderdale?"

Thorn looked at his former agents and calmly counseled them to, "Put down your weapons, men. Your revolution is over, and you lost. I'll make sure you have good attorneys and, if you surrender peacefully, I'll put in good words for both of you."

"Shut up, Thorn!" Sane spat. "There's a treasure in this building and we want it! If we get what we want, we'll lock all of you in a room and leave quietly. No one has to die."

"It's Christmas Eve, guys," I said. "We don't have any treasure here. We don't even have any loose change. There are a couple of beers in the fridge if you're interested."

Sane was getting a little squirrelly and I thought he might just start shooting at any minute. And I not only didn't want to see anyone shot, I didn't want to see any of the framed classic movie posters splattered or blasted by those assholes.

"You're time travelers!" he screamed. "Winston said that! Where's your time machine?"

Thorn looked at Sane like the man's last name was no longer descriptive.

"You got us, Agent Sane," I said. "We didn't know you were in the loop on our scientific achievements."

"This is ridiculous!" Thorn spat, just before Curruthers hit him over the head with his Glock. The good-guy agent dropped to the floor.

"Hey," I said. "No need for that. We'll show you the time machine."

"Is that how Prof. Winston escaped?" Sane asked.

"Exactly," I said. "We made a very good deal with Winston. The professor is currently enjoying himself in his own castle on the Rhine in 1852. He had traveled to Gold Strike, California in 1849 and, knowing where to dig, struck it rich. Then he traveled a couple of years into the future with his riches and purchased a small empire."

In my head, I sounded pretty stupid as I made everything up while my lips continued to flap. But it made sense to the two commie idiots who had listened a little too much to Winston.

"How do you know?" Curruthers asked.

"We sent him there," I said. "We've been to the past and the future. Winston figured out the treasure was the ability to move back in time with today's knowledge."

"I want to see it!" Sane said. "The machine!"

"And so you shall," I said. "Let's leave Agent Thorn to sleep a bit while we go to the time machine."

While my lips continued to move and I blithered about time travel, I started walking down the hall with Buck, Sky, Zack and the two traitors. Lucky followed quietly. My impromptu act continued, even though I felt like I had been shoved onto a karaoke stage, but no one was faking my voice. We turned and entered the conference room.

"Come in," I said. "Just be careful what you touch."

The two men were impressed by the amazing conference room, which looked like Capt. Kirk and the crew of the Starship Enterprise belonged there.

"Now we," I motioned toward my friends, "are going to stand right here against the wall in front of you while I demonstrate the amazing modern miracle of time travel. And if you men would just take a seat facing us, I am going to show you something you never thought possible."

"No tricks! If you pull something shady, we'll blast every one of you!" Sane threatened.

"No tricks," I explained. "If you look at my friend right here, you'll see that we have brought cowboy movie star Buck Jones from the past into our 21st Century world."

The two morons looked closely at Buck.

"Well, Howdy," the big ham said.

"I've never seen any of Jones' movies," Sane stated.

"I saw a few of them years ago on television," Curruthers added. "He looks like that dude."

"For my first demonstration, I'm going to bring someone into this room from the past who you will immediately know," I said. "Would that be okay with you guys?"

"Who you gonna bring?" Sane asked.

"I'm thinking I'll dial up a superstar who everyone can recognize," I said. "And I'm going to snatch him right off the set of his 1950s television show."

I reached to the table and picked up a ballpoint pen in my right hand.

"Now, please pull an empty chair between you," I said, directing the two dumbasses. "That's right. Our visitor will appear in that chair."

Lucky smiled at me, winked and moved to his designated position.

"This may look like a simple writing pen," I said. "But it isn't. It's a time-ramifications capacitor, which I have preset to reach out to Iverson Ranch in Chatsworth, California back in 1958. So when I push this button, our visitor from the past will be swooped up from way back then and dropped in that chair between you."

The two commies' eyes were bugged wide as they listened to my claptrap.

"Now, please stay calm."

Both men focused their eyes on the ballpoint pen in my hand. With a very serious expression on my face, I reached upward, pointed the pen toward the "empty" chair, and pushed the button. Lucky, already seated between the thugs, used his elbows to slightly touch the two gullible morons. The bright light flashed in front of them and both of their jaws dropped when they saw Steve McQueen, as Josh Randall from "Wanted Dead or Alive," appear between them.

"Holy shit!" Sane yelled.

At that exact moment, Lucky smashed him in the side of his head with the butt of his mare's leg. Curruthers didn't make out too well either, as the wraith pulled the trigger on his sawed-off Winchester, blasting smoke and a loud bang in his face. The temporarily deaf agent, thinking his head had been blown off, fainted forward onto the table.

I dived toward them and snatched their Glocks, handing one to Buck while keeping the men covered.

"You had me confused for a few minutes, Dave," Zack said.

"It surprises me that those two morons were able to become federal agents," Sky said. "But they certainly fit in with the rest of the People's Brigade toadies."

Buck and I used the agents' own handcuffs to secure them while Sky and Zack went to aid Agent Thorn. Curruthers was the first to regain consciousness. He seemed extremely confused, and this didn't improve when, Lucky, who had adopted the look of Strother Martin from "Cool Hand Luke," looked down at him and said, "What we've got here is failure to communicate." Then the over-acting wraith struck the man across his face with a leather-wrapped club.

I looked over at Lucky and, as quietly as possible, whispered, "Don't overdo it with the movie theme."

Once Sane opened his eyes, we yanked both men to their feet. Buck pulled his Dodgers cap tightly on his head and smiled at the dazed thugs.

"Start walkin', boys," he said. "Let's just hope your former boss will recover from your assault."

When we got to the lobby, I saw that Zack had helped Agent Thorn into a comfortable reception room chair. The fed was seated with a can of beer in his hand, while Sky gently used a wet washcloth to clean around his wounded noggin.

"How're you doing, agent?" I asked.

"I'll live."

Not very gently, we shoved the two traitors onto their knees.

"I'm sorry to tell you that not only are these two wastes of oxygen traitors, but I think they have serious drug problems," I explained.

"He's lyin', boss!" Sane yelled. "He brought Steve McQueen from 1958!"

"What the hell?" Thorn gasped.

"Hold still, agent," Sky said, with one hand on his shoulder and the other still dabbing at his head wound. "You don't want to start bleeding again."

"It's the truth!" Sane babbled. "And he hit me in the head with that sawed-off gun of his!"

I just shook my head sadly. "These two are flyin' pretty high."

"That bounty-hunter cowboy shot me in the face!" Curruthers added, then pointed at Buck. "And that's Buck Jones!"

The big cowboy grinned like Joe E. Brown with the brim of his baseball cap flipped up.

"Yeah," I explained. "He got the idea that Charlie was an old cowboy who had made silent movies."

"C'mon, boss!" Curruthers yelled. "Strother Martin hit me just like he did Paul Newman in that movie! And Steve McQueen is standing right over there!"

The enemy agent pointed to an "empty" area of the room.

"I don't know if these dumb clucks are preparing an insanity defense or if they're just stoned to the gills," I said. "But the sooner you can get them out of here, the happier we will be."

Agent Thorn pulled his cellphone from his shirt pocket as he stood up, slowly, and called for backup to come fetch the traitors.

"Zack," Thorn said. "I don't know how to apologize to you and your team for this. I'm just so ashamed that this happened."

"Don't be," Zack said. "The enemy has found ways to thrust its tentacles into the foundations of our democracy. I think you and all good members of law enforcement are the cure for this invasive disease. And I'm just glad we uncovered these drug-addled traitors before they were able to cause any more harm."

"Just don't let any crooked attorneys get these guys off on an 'innocent due to insanity' plea," I said.

Invisible Josh Randall stood over the two kneeling turncoats with his tongue darting in and out, as he rapidly moved his hands around their heads, pinching their noses and poking them.

"Get him off! Go away!" Curruthers screamed.

"Stop it! Get off of me!" Sane stuttered, with tears running out of his eyes.

"Such a sad case," Zack said as he shook his head. "Nancy Reagan was right. Perhaps if these two had just said…"

And right on cue, Curruthers yelled, "No!"

Ten minutes later a dark van pulled up outside. Two NSA agents helped Thorn chain the Looney Tune traitors inside the back, ready for transport.

"Everyday presents a new surprise," Thorn said. "I'm going to recommend an internal investigation to make sure we can rid ourselves of any and all enemies that may have assumed a deep cover within our agency."

Thorn climbed into the van passenger seat and waved.

"Watch your back," Zack said.

We returned to the lobby and, unanimously, followed Zack to the beer fridge.

"Agent Thorn never did get around to any real questions about Watkins," Sky said. "At least he now realizes the missing agent was also a Quisling."

"Once again," Zack said. "That man has a lot on his plate."

"Hey," I added. "The good news is, this time we don't have any heavy duty cleanups to perform."

We decided it was a good time to knock off work so we could accomplish some last-minute preparation for Christmas.

●●●

We were due at my sister's home at four on Christmas day, and it looked like we'd be right on time. Zack, wearing a red sweater with three green Christmas trees and two black Bigfoot silhouettes on it, drove us in his amazing 1940 Ford Deluxe Station Wagon. Buck, wearing his Rough Riders western clothing rode shotgun. In the middle seat, I wore my usual western wear along with my new white Stetson while I snuggled up with Sky, who sparkled in a light blue dress with a burgundy sweater that sported a cartoon reindeer with unusually large horns. In the backseat, Josh Randall, minus his mare's leg, grinned and looked ready to party.

Linda had strung several lines of Christmas lights on her porch, as well as a big green wreath on her door. An inflated Santa tied to the porch swing bobbed in the slight breeze. My mind began to become slightly judgmental concerning the blow up St. Nicholas until I noticed the line of eight inflated reindeer hanging upside down off the neighbor's rain gutter.

"What a lovely home," Sky said.

"Wait until you get inside," I stated, as I knocked.

Linda opened the door and I watched, while her eyes seemed to enlarge with each introduction.

"Gang. This is my sister, Linda. Linda, meet the most wonderful, beautiful lady in the world, Sky Blue."

Sky blushed as she placed the three apple pies she was carrying on a side table and hugged Linda, who whispered in her ear, "Is Dave sane?"

"Close enough for government work," Sky smiled.

"And this is Prof. Zack Delaney," I said. "He's a smart cookie."

She shook his hand as he entered.

"Where would you like the beer?" Zack asked.

"Just put the cases on the kitchen table," she said. "I'll get 'em in the ice chests."

Buck and I set our cases on the floor to take into the kitchen after introductions.

"I know you still think I'm crazy, but this is Buck Jones," I said.

She looked up at the tall cowboy and became momentarily speechless.

"It's so nice to meet all of you," she then stammered. "This is my son, Sammy."

"Buck Jones!" Sammy exclaimed. "Howdy!"

Buck dropped to one knee and shook Sammy's hand. "Proud to meetcha, Sammy."

"Gee, Buck," my nephew said. "I wish your partners Tim and Sandy were here too."

"So do I, Sammy. But I'm ridin' with a new crew these days. And when it comes to fightin' for justice, your uncle Dave is a pretty darn good partner as well."

"I'm sorry your friend Lucky didn't make it," Linda said.

"Oh, he's here," Sky said.

I watched as Lucky walked into the house, closed the door behind him and touched Linda and Sammy's shoulders. My sister started to drop to the floor when she saw Josh Randall, but Buck caught her. "Gotcha, ma'am. And, yes, that's Lucky. Apparently he looks like an actor I've never heard of from a few years back."

"Wow!" Sammy yelled. "That's some trick! This is gonna be great! We've got a Rough Rider and an ace magician for Christmas!"

Linda looked into my eyes and asked, "So everything you told me was true?"

"Yep."

"And you really did go back to 1942 and bring Mr. Jones back with you?"

"Yes, ma'am."

"And all this craziness I'm seein' on the news is because of you and the video you told me you made?"

"That's a fact."

"And ghosts, dragons and banshees are real?"

"And Bigfoot!" I answered.

"Mom," Sammy said. "The timer just went off in the kitchen."

"Everyone," Linda said. "I am so happy you're here. Welcome to our home. Please forgive me if I stutter or seem a little shocked. This is just so amazing to me. I know I've always dreamed of a magical Christmas and, voila, here we are." She giggled. "Dinner will be ready in about twenty minutes. Dave. Please get everyone something to drink."

I didn't have to ask. I went to one of the ice chests and retrieved cold bottles of beer for Sky, Buck, Zack, Lucky and myself, and a root beer for Sammy. Linda had gone back into the kitchen to continue dinner preparations. I delivered the drinks and then stuck my head through the kitchen door and asked, "Are you okay?"

"I'm good, Dave," Linda said. "My mind is digesting what I just witnessed and I'm, surprisingly, calm. In fact, I'm happy and I can't explain it."

"Happiness doesn't need an explanation, Linda. Just go with it."

I rejoined the others in time to enjoy one of Lucky's funny historical stories.

"You'll excuse me a moment," Zack said. "I forgot something in the car."

He went outside and returned moments later with a stack of wrapped packages, which he placed under the lighted Christmas tree as we all gathered in the living room. Linda came back in from the kitchen. The scientist sat down on a plush chair and addressed us all.

"Linda. I am grateful for your invitation to join you today, of all days. This Christmas is probably more special than any other, except the first one. You see, without the bravery of your brother, there would be no Christmas this year. Without the great knowledge and faith of my brilliant assistant, Sky Blue, there would be no holidays ever again. Without the strength and resolute courage of war veteran and classic western star Buck Jones, violence and chaos would be the only thing we would have left. And without our very special friend Lucky, all civilization would no longer exist. These heroes are the Sundance team."

Lucky whispered in my ear, "Is this where I'm supposed to sing the 'Battle Hymn of the Republic'?"

"No."

"We were kind of busy lately, so I didn't get a chance to do any real Christmas shopping," Zack continued. "But I brought a few last-minute token items that I would like you to accept."

"I didn't see any of these packages in the Ford," I said.

"I had them behind the backseat," he answered.

The scientist handed a document to Sky. "I have to announce a spoiler alert because this was to be a New Year's surprise. You have been such a big part of our research and discoveries over the years and this is long overdue. You now are a complete partner, half owner, in everything at Sundance Laboratories. Thank you for all your efforts, partner."

Sky looked at the agreement and, with tears in her eyes, hugged the red bearded scientist.

Zack handed Buck a small package to unwrap.

"What is it?" the cowboy asked.

"An iPhone," Zack said. "You're now a 21st Century champion of justice. This will help."

Buck looked at it and said, "Thanks. I've been wondering about not seeing any payphones. Of course, you're gonna have to teach me how to use this thing.

I especially need to know how to contact the long distance operator."

The scientist then handed Sammy a box. "I understand you're a pretty good reader."

"I am," Sammy answered, while removing the wrapping and opening the box.

"Those are Buck Jones comic books and Big Little Books that I have collected over the years," Zack explained. "If you're going to be a member of the Sundance team, you're going to need to learn about the cowboy hero you'll be riding with."

"Yeehaw!" Sammy said. "Hear that, Mom?"

"I did," Linda answered. "And, from now on I think I'll join you and your uncle at the Old Timer Theatre for those matinees."

"I'll be there as well," Buck announced.

"Dave can't go without me," Sky added. "I get my best rest during those movies."

"Lucky," Zack said. "You are just amazing at everything you do. I couldn't find any physical item that I thought you might need. So I am having a sound stage built at the labs so you can play your music, record your music and, even though you are an expert at recreating other people's recordings, you may even be able to create your own sound that you could release to the public."

"You know," Lucky said. "That's not a bad idea. I never thought about making my own music."

Then, without saying anything, Zack handed me a large flat wrapped package. When I unwrapped it, my mouth opened and I was flabbergasted. It was a framed original movie poster of George Pal's 1960 classic, "The Time Machine," just like the one in Zack's office.

"It just seemed appropriate," he said.

"Thanks!" I hollered like I was ten years old. "That's amazing!"

"And Linda," Zack said. "You are so gracious to have us here today. Dave tells me you are an accountant. Sundance Labs currently needs a fulltime accountant. And if you are interested, we'd like you to join us."

"How do you know I'll be any good?"

"Trust me," I said. "Zack has checked you out."

"And we pay twice what you are making."

Linda had sat through almost a dozen amazing surprises since we arrived, but the job offer set her stammering. "Ah, um, yes! Yes! Wonderful!"

"And this is for you," Zack said, handing her a flat gift about the size of a phonebook.

Wide-eyed and giggly like a teenager, Linda tore the wrapping paper off and smiled. "I love it!"

She held up a framed black and white signed photo of Gail Davis as "Annie Oakley."

Lucky's guitar showed up out of nowhere and he began to sing "Back in the Saddle Again" in Gene Autry's voice. What was unnerving was that, so he wouldn't confuse Sammy, he stayed in his Steve McQueen image.

Sky pulled me aside and we walked to the back porch where we could be alone.

"We have certainly been very busy," she said. "And I haven't had the chance to go shopping."

"Me either," I said, sheepishly.

"But this is an amazing Christmas and I want to give you a piece of my heart," she whispered, as she pulled me close and kissed me on the lips, sending more electricity through my body than would have been available from the late Stanley's backpack, harpoon, industrial-strength Laser. The lights that flashed in my mind were brighter than those created by the time machine, and the warmth that flowed between us was far superior to a blazing campfire. We held that pose for quite a while, with our arms wrapped tightly around each other.

I pulled my head back an inch or two and looked her in the eyes.

"Now that you are my boss at Sundance, I hope you won't write me up for this," I said, nuzzling her neck. "I need to tell you that if I'm going to be involved in any more time travel, it better be to the past. Because you are my future."

We held each other and professed our love for the next several minutes until Sky stepped back and said, "We better go back in there before Lucky drinks all the beer."

We returned to the warm, happy living room with pink-cheeked blushes that we didn't attempt to hide.

"Hey," Linda hollered. "Let's eat."

We all meandered into the dining room to find our seats at the large, oval, Queen Anne dining table. Sky sat close to my left, while Sammy was on my right, next to Buck. On the other side of Sky were Zack, then Lucky and Linda between him and Buck. In the middle of the table my amazing sister had placed a large prime rib roast, already sliced. Two big bowls containing hot baked potatoes adorned the tablecloth, while warm homemade bread loaves sat on cutting blocks at each end of the table. We all gazed at the wonderful feast and then looked at each other with the age-old holiday question, "Who's going to say grace?"

"Well I know it's not karaoke," our friendly, magnificent, sometimes-invisible, time-traveling spirit said. "But I think I can handle this."

I tried not to dwell on the concept, as I bowed my head.

"Father in Heaven," he prayed. "Please bless this meal and all of my wonderful friends at this table. And thank you for blessing our sometimes-confrontational efforts to protect the innocent. Please forgive us if we enjoyed the confrontational part too much. Thank you for our health and our happiness. And thank you for bringing Dave and Sky together, because," and he changed his speaking pattern to that of a school-yard smartass, "they are in love!" Sky giggled while I smirked. Then Lucky looked up to the ceiling and said, "Thank you for life."

We happily chowed down as we shared that delicious meal, as well as a lot of stories and bushels of laughs. When it came time for the apple pie, Lucky excused himself so he could find a seat and serenade us with Bing Crosby songs from "White Christmas," which was wonderful but slightly odd coming out of Steve McQueen's mouth.

All things combined, I would say I had more fun that Christmas than I ever had before. As my sister so aptly said earlier, it was magical.

The next week was fairly smooth as Zack and Sky tinkered on the time level equipment; while I attempted to teach Buck how to get on the Internet. His question was, of course, "Why?" I remember how proud he was when he received his first call on his iPhone. "It's a man who's telling me he's been trying to reach me concerning my vehicle's warranty!" Lessons continued.

Lucky assisted Linda on background checks for potential new employees, in that we needed to hire a receptionist and a lab assistant. We had a few scheduling meetings, but things were pretty loosey-goosey, in that it was almost New Year's. Sky and I had planned to party like it was 1999 on New Year's Eve.

When we weren't working, Lucky stayed at my place. He made the La-Z-Boy recliner his main hangout. Mostly, we had a pretty good time watching sports and old western movies on television. About the only problem we had was when one of the neighbors came by to complain about how much he hated the "lousy hillbilly music" that was always playing in my house and that if I didn't silence it, he would call the police. And the next day he did call the police, not to report us but to demand help because his German shepherd wouldn't stop singing Hank Williams songs. Law enforcement found some caring people who took the neighbor someplace where he could find some peace and quiet, while animal control representatives picked up the dog with the hopes of finding it a new, sane owner.

On the morning of December 31, 2022, I woke up to the sound of a rumbling on the front porch.

"Damn bikers!" I sputtered.

I sat up, put on my robe and slippers and staggered into the front room. Lucky stood looking out the window with a cup of steaming coffee in his hand. I walked toward him.

"You want some coffee?" he asked.

"No! What's all this racket goin' on?"

"Dave. Have you ever heard the one where the Indian, the dragon and the banshee walk into a bar?"

"No! And why would you wake me up to ask me that?"

He sauntered to the front door and opened it. Standing on the porch was our friendly tribal spirit in front of a gigantic green dragon, which looked up at me sheepishly knowing it had knocked over a couple of potted plants. Hovering over them both was the big, white, fearsome banshee.

"It looks like there's big trouble at the ranch," the musical wraith said.

"And there goes my New Year's Eve!" I spat.

THE END

ABOUT OUR CREATORS

WRITER & ARTIST -

DARRYLE PURCELL has had a variety of jobs during his lifetime—including soldier, illustrator, editorial cartoonist, newspaper managing editor and government flack.

He served in the Army as an infantry paratrooper in the First Cavalry Division in Vietnam and then stateside as a medic, first in the 101st Airborne Division, then in the 82nd Airborne Division. Following the military, he worked his way through college, graduating with an art degree from Cal State University Long Beach, which led to a career as a cartoonist in magazines, newspapers, educational comic books and Saturday morning animated television shows.

Purcell's political cartoons garnered quite a few awards in California during the 1980s and early '90s, while his work as a newspaper managing editor in the later '90s and first few years of the new century led to many statewide awards in Arizona for news columns and editorials. From 2005 through 2012, he was a public information director for a county in Arizona.

Purcell currently writes and illustrates the "Hollywood Cowboy Detectives," "Man of the Mist" and "Vermin" pulp adventures from his home in rural Arizona, where he lives with his wife Patricia. A collection of his newspaper columns and cartoons from the last 30 years titled "Hell to Humor" has also recently been published. The new "Buck Jones in the 21st Century" book for Airship 27 is a reflection of his love of the classic B-westerns of the 1930s through the 1950s, while dealing with contemporary issues of our modern society.

A SECOND GO-ROUND

James Francis sits on a bar stool the night of his 65th birthday reflecting on his sad life. He grew up hating his father, married the wrong girl and was soon divorced. He never had any children or close friends and now he's alone facing his twilight years. Bitter memories are his sole companions. Or so he believes until he is approached by a funny little man who suggest that he might be able to go back and re-live his life—a second time. Only with one major difference. This time he would make the right decisions. If that were at all possible, would he accept the offer?

And thus begins R.A. Jones' wonderful tale of a man miraculously given a second chance at life. It is a poignant story that reveals the significance of every choice we make along the journey. Each choice having endless cause and effect to shape the person we will ultimately become. As for James Francis, his do-over is one filled with love, heartache and forgiveness no reader will ever forget.

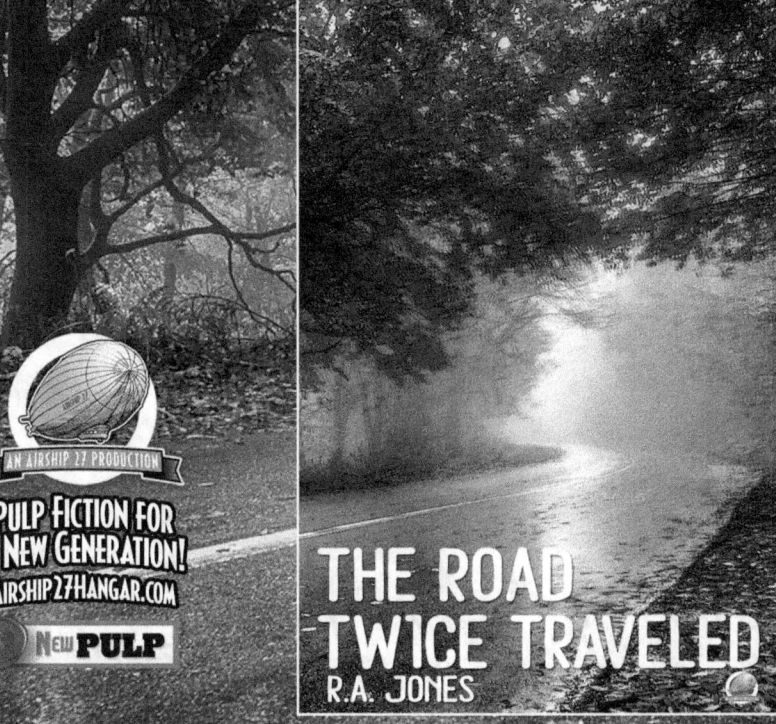

AN AIRSHIP 27 PRODUCTION

PULP FICTION FOR A NEW GENERATION!
AIRSHIP27HANGAR.COM

NEW PULP

THE ROAD TWICE TRAVELED
R.A. JONES

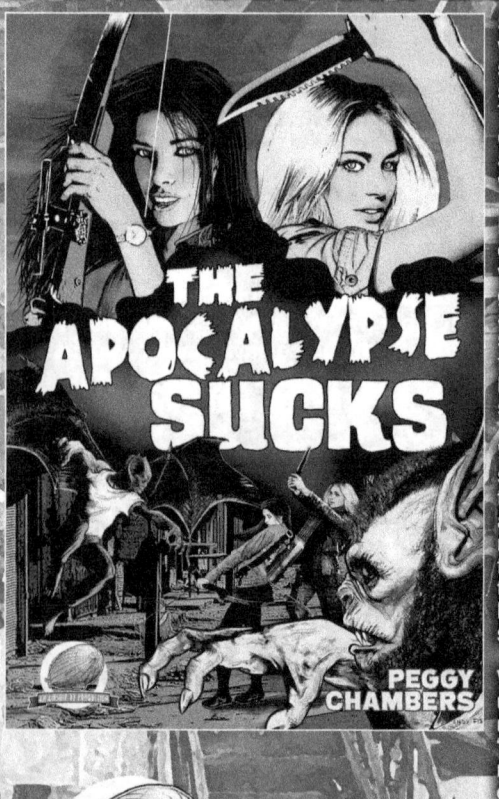

www.ingramcontent.com/pod-product-compliance
Lightning Source LLC
Chambersburg PA
CBHW051150260626
47170CB00005B/2041